RISING AFRICAN PATRIOTS

Other books by the author

Fear Not, Child (2014)

Roses in the Mines (2017)

RISING AFRICAN PATRIOTS

Gabriel S. Makeri

ISBN: 978-978-55613-3-3

National Library of Nigeria Cataloguing-in-Publication Data

Printed and Published in Nigeria by:
Words Rhymes & Rhythm Limited
Suite C309, Global Plaza Plot 366,
ObafemiAwolowo Way, Jabi District, Abuja, Nigeria.
08169027757, 08060109295
www.wrr.ng

DEDICATION

This book is dedicated to:

Africa's founding fathers,

Mo Ibrahim, the Sudanese – British, who cares for, and encourages, good leadership in Africa.

Alhaji Aliko Dangote,
who has invested in many African countries, boosting the African economy.

Prof. Patrick Loch Otieno Lumumba,
whose heart bleeds profusely because of the underdevelopment of Africa and,

all LOVERS of Africa.

ACKNOWLEDGEMENTS

I appreciate the following people for taking time to go through this work and making some observations, corrections and suggestions: Dr. Ayuba S. Buru, Alhaji Ahmed Umar Chawai, Mrs. Gladys A. Goje, Chief Danbaba T. Tukura, Mr. Yahya Attari Bala, Mr. Alabi Isaac Ade, Mr. Abba Abubakar Kabara, Mr. Muhammad Sabiu, Dr. A. A. Kura, Dr. Suleiman Sa'adu Matazu, Mr. Bulus Dogara Emishe, Professor Ntim Gyakari Esew, Engr. Mailafia Isaac, Mr. Daniel Adejo, Mr. Samson A. Anduwa, Dr. Sani Adamu, and Elder Benjamin Zego. Thank you all.

My wife— Naomi; the children: Eguro, Jemimah, La'itu and Salome for their moral support. I appreciate my father, late Papa Eguro (Sarkin Makera) and my mother, late Cibi Eguro (a. k. a Kyau) for their commitment to my upbringing. Thanks, indeed.

Thanks to Emmanuel Isah and Matthew Sunday, for typing this work.

And to God, for the inspiration, the insight, the energy, and the resources given me for the success of this work; to Him alone be boundless praise and glory.

All the names of characters appearing in this book save for historical figures and contemporary personalities such as Mo Ibrahim, Alh. Aliko Dangote and Prof. Patrick Loch Otieno Lumumba and others in quoted papers, are fictionally used. This also applies to some names of places such as New York.

COMMENTS

"Amazing; this novel describes the concept of mind renaissance through positive optimism that all souls were created equal. It also highlights the essence that freedom from all forms of subjugation starts from within."

—Ayuba S. Buru, PhD, *Faculty of Medicine, Department of Pathology, Kaduna State University, Kaduna, Nigeria*

ꙮ

"Mr. Makeri is a trained miner and has a VISION for PATRIOTISM for the emancipation of Africa. In a simple narration using history, geography, international relations, religion, etc, he tries to inculcate in people the importance of PATRIOTISM with all the sacrifices contained therein where in the end it will remove selfishness, religious and tribal bigotry which are some of the causes of underdevelopment of the African continent. I recommend this novel for both the YOUNG and the OLD, especially the YOUNG in their formative years."

—Alhaji Ahmed Umar Chawai, *Former Director General, Ministry of Finance and, Former Permanent Commissioner, Local Govt. Service Commission, Kaduna State, Nigeria*

ꙮ

"The Rising African Patriots" is a must-read for all. Although this is fiction, in a simple narrative style Elder Makeri has succeeded in showing that God is mindful of Nigeria in particular and Africa in general. There is still hope for Africa. It is not yet over until God says so. Africa's lost glory can be restored if all hands are on deck. The choice is ours. God will not come down from heaven and do what we should do. The answer lies with us. If every man, woman and child decides to be patriotic rather self-centered, the light of patriotism will surely pierce the darkness Africa has been plunged into. God will then spread His healing hands across the continent and heal us. The journey of a thousand miles starts with just one step, that step must be taken by you and me now."

— Gladys A. Goje (Mrs.), *Principal Lecturer, Department of Languages, Kaduna Polytechnic, Kaduna, Nigeria*

ཏ

"The novel, Rising African Patriots, is not only about patriotism but has also elucidated the socio-political history, environment, economy, geography and resourcefulness of mother Africa in general terms."

— Yahaya Attayi Bala, *Zonal Coordinator, North-West Zone, Nigeria Geological Survey Agency (NGSA), Sokoto*

ཏ

"This very interesting novel narrates the activities and achievements of African past patriots. The author tells his readers in an explicit tone what it takes to be patriotic. The author advocates in strong terms for the need of the spirit of patriotism by African leaders and the led. I hereby recommend the book to all and sundries aspiring to be patriotic and be examples worthy of emulation by future generations."

— Alabi, Isaac Ade, *Chief Education Officer (rtd), Federal Govt. Girl's College, Kazaure, Jigawa State, Nigeria*

ཏ

"This is a refreshing novel on patriotism. The author attempts to narrate a patriot's penchant desire to see his people liberated from unpatriotism and neo-colonialism. Even though the major character eventually died, other patriots continue with the struggle to see the continent, Africa, attains greatness."

— Muhammad Sabiu, *(Dan Malikin S/Garin Kakuri), Northern Bureau Chief, Nigerian Tribune, Kaduna, Nigeria*

ཏ

"After a careful reading of the manuscript of this novel which is divided into twelve chapters, I became very interested on the direction and ideas of the author. This book is good for those who will be willing to become patriots if they are not already. It also serves as a collection of ideas which if used will help to develop a passion for patriotism in the minds of the younger generation of African youths. To the general public, this book... will be a guide to selecting leaders at all levels for Africa.

"I therefore recommend that this book should be read by all and sundry."

— A. A. Kura, PhD, *Lecturer (rtd), Ahmadu Bello University, Zaria, Nigeria*

ꕥ

"Other continents of the world are struggling to keep their regions flying through raising good patriots. Africa should not be left out in this direction. Thus, the Rising African Patriots by Makeri is timely. It is a book that will ginger Africans to stand up and be true patriots of their continent. Having gone through the manuscript, the simplicity with which it is written is incredible and commendable. I therefore recommend this novel for use by individuals and schools."

— Suleiman Sa'adu Matazu, PhD, *Department of Science and Vocational Education, Faculty of Education and Extension Services, Usman Danfodiyo University, Sokoto, Nigeria*

ꕥ

"Have you even been bothered of the great need for your country to be made great and be so respected by other countries? Have you bothered how that is to be attained in your life time? Have you ever given a thought that you can be that great agent through whom your country can attain greatness in its true sense and be so respected? What is that in you that can bring such a change? Are you aware that patriotism is that factor? Kindly go through this write-up and it will amaze you what patriotism is all about."

— Bulus DogaraEmishe, *Permanent Secretary (rtd) and Serving Special Adviser on*

Economic and Budget Matters to the Governor, Kaduna State, Nigeria

ꕥ

"The Rising African Patriots even though prose, is an in-depth study which touches on the 'Saints' of Africa whose exemplary lives must be emulated by the younger generation. It is a novel which is recommended not only as a text for the classroom but also for all Africans who really want to be patriotic."

— Professor Ntim Gyakari Esew, *Department of Political Science, Kaduna State University, Kaduna, Nigeria*

ꕥ

"This book is a demonstration of the writer's ability and talent in creative writing. It is a wake-up call to Africans and their heads of government to rise up to the challenges of moving the African continent to greater heights. It should be adopted by African union and be recommended to all schools."

— Mailafia Isaac, *Communication Engineer, Kaduna Electricity Distribution Company, Nigeria*

ꕥ

"Makeri has in this book precisely encapsulated the bane of African underdevelopment which he aptly called unpatriotism. For everyone that is concerned about the sorry state of Africa, he has found a compatriot in Makeri. A study of his mind as conveyed in this book will galvanize a movement that will move Africa to where it should be. So, African patriots, make this book a companion."

— Samson A. Anduwa, *FCA, Fellow of the Institute of Chartered Accountants of Nigeria (ICAN).*

ꕥ

"The Rising African Patriots by Makeri is timely, especially in this critical period where emphasis must be on nation building and economic integration among nations."

— Sani Adamu, PhD, *Directorate of Peace Keeping and Regional Security, ECOWAS Commission, Abuja, Nigeria.*

ꕤ

"In this book the author is strongly advocating for deliberate effort to promote patriotism among Africans. Africans have had the taste of patriotism from our founding fathers who displayed their genuine love for Africa. Even though most of them are dead, they should serve as mentors to the present generation of Africans. To the author, blacks are unique with abilities to achieve in any field of endeavour as their white counterparts if not more. Therefore, I recommend this book to all lovers of Africa and to African governments to adopt it as a curriculum text in schools in order to breed patriots."

— Elder Benjamin B. Zego, *Theologian/Manager, Spring Aluminum Nigeria limited, Kaduna.*

ꕤ

"Rising African Patriots portrays a striking attempt by the author to motivate a renaissance of the lost values in the culture of originality, by presenting a well-researched, a very graphic account of beliefs, philosophies, and spirit of patriotism, clearly defined vision and selflessness demonstrated by the Africa's past heroes to promote the unity of African states. The book is a cynosure of inspirations for our contemporary African leaders to draw a retrospective analysis on the values and philosophies of those great leaders and to enable them work towards the rebirth of another era of nationalism for the desired unity and socio-economic freedom of African states.

I would strongly suggest that the final copy of this striking intellectual work be recommended for studies in our tertiary institutions.

— Abba Abubakar Kabara, *Regional Editor, North West, Leadership Newspapers, Gusau, Nigeria*

ꕤ

ONE

ഇ

"Julius! Julius! Julius! Oh my God! Julius, are you dreaming?" Matthew screamed at his long time friend who seemed to be daydreaming. Both men were born on the same day in their village Pa, in southern Kaduna, though Matthew arrived an hour earlier than Julius.

Julius was a commercial farmer and teacher who was passionate about nationalist activism and patriotism. He was internationally acclaimed due to his regular contributions on politics and patriotism in a reputable and globally read monthly magazine. He had visited a number of countries to deliver lectures at conferences. He taught at one of the secondary schools in Kaduna before he left for Pa on transfer, leaving behind the office he used for his campaigns and patriotic activities.

Matthew was his friend and disciple. He taught in the same school as Julius and was also popular for his patriotic activities, having represented Julius at several international conferences.

Julius developed a sudden likeness for Pa ever since he learnt that patriots used to gather in the village as a form of a pilgrimage. The gathering was organized during the colonial era to give lectures on patriotism and nationalism in honor of his maternal grandfather, a patriot revered even by foreigners.

Pa was a prominent village hedged by rocky hills to the north, east and south, with a slightly elevated ridge of laterite sloping gently to the plains of the village by the west. A tarred road from the west cut through Pa to another village in a dense forest.The road was an off-set from the Kaduna–Abuja dual carriage highway, giving the people easy access to the Federal Capital of Nigeria.

Julius visited Abuja every now and then and enjoyed seeing the undulating terrain of the capital city which lies in a depression when viewed from Mpape hills in the northern part of the city. When appreciating the topography of the land, his heart skipped in dire longing that the plains be peopled daily by patriots like him.

From the northern part of Pa where a jagged hill nurtured green vegetation was a beautiful spring cascading in a trifecta of rippling tides. The thick forest which used to be home to monkeys and some wild animals ate deep into the fringes of the village in absolute quietude. The animals had been hunted into near extinction by village hunters.

This spring had long been a tourist site, even though the villagers still saw it as their only reliable source of water. They drank from the spring for as long as they could remember. The founding fathers settled for the place and it offered them protection against enemies, especially during the days of inter-tribal wars that ravaged Africa. At a foothill of one of Pa's many imposing hills, was where the patriots used to gather to receive lectures and discuss on patriotism and Africa's nationalism. Julius had been shown the site for this ritual by his maternal grandfather, and he frequented it to have an imaginary feel of that period.

The vastness of the hills in the village was so intimidating that it scared little children and weakly men. Only strong adults and old men who grew up taking *jiko*, a local energy drink made from assorted roots and barks of trees ended up being able to reach the hilltops. Stories told of old patriots said they ascended the brow of the hill shortly after independence to seek God's face so patriotism could reign in the land and all over Africa. Julius, who felt like a patriot in every way, had been to the hilltops too, seeking God's face.

Jiko made farmers work untiringly, warm steam escaping their coarse skin as they glided rhythmically from one ridge to the other, tilling the soil. It also drove the misty morning cold away, even under the rain. Even now, it does. The farmers, having taken the *jiko*, usually got so overwhelmed in tilling the soil while chanting glorious songs of antiquity; they hardly noticed how long they had overstayed in the farm. The *jiko* was usually left to ferment for two weeks or more. It stayed so long that bacteria fed on it and welcomed all sorts of germs. Despite how unclean the *jiko* turned, ancestors rebuked children for trying to pick out germs before drinking. '*It should be taken wholly with the germs in it*', they would insist. Removal of germs would weaken the potency of the *jiko*. For them, it was patriotic upholding ancient customs and traditions. And in fact, there had never been any reported case of sickness from taking germs infested *jiko*; rather it gave more strength to consumers. Julius learnt of the efficacy of *jiko* and prepared it every month during the rainy season after he was taught how to prepare it.

If not for the traversing streams and rivers, plain lands would have lain untroubled by water bodies and green vegetation. River Wild glided densely towards the north-south direction. The profile of River Wild was rough with boulders, causing menacing waves during rainy season. It is apparently at an equidistant from the foot of the hills by the east and a mound of laterite with round pebbles to its west. Folktales had it that the caves in the lateritic region were once inhabited by lions.

It was from the caves that the lions occasionally prowled into the village to disrupt its peace. Many goats had been raided by these carnivorous beasts and even people too—four villagers were found lifeless in the bush with dismembered limbs and ripped parts. The lions had suddenly disappeared and no one took notice when and where their present habitat is. Which man hates his life so much that he goes prying lions? The abandoned caves had long been inhabited by reptiles some of which, like the python, are very dangerous.

A hunter in the village said he saw a giant python creeping out of the cave some few years ago. He had dished out unbelievable tales of how he fought the python and pierced him with his sword before he escaped into the thick forest. He told all he knew about pythons and made the rest up and he was celebrated for some months in the village for fighting a python which we all know could kill and swallow humans. Since the escapades, the area had been fearfully avoided by villagers, and strangers had been warned from going to the caves.

"Julius!" Matthew called again even though Julius wasn't answering. In a sort of a trance, Julius' spirit seemed to have left his body for a distant land. He was seated near an artificial pond which had been the main source of laterite in the village.

Matthew called again, clapping so he could grab Julius' attention, but Julius was still unresponsive, even to croaking frogs in the pond and termites moving ceaselessly in and out of an anthill close to them.

He sighed and moved towards him; nudging him on the elbow, he asked, "What is the problem with you?" Julius ignored him. The coldness was unusual.

"I have been watching you for a while. You seemed carried away. What is it with you?"

Julius swayed his head forward, resting it on his cupped palms which are supported by his elevated ankles. He writhed in discomfort as he balanced his bottom upon a polished piece of granitic rock.

His countenance was gloomy and his eyes weary. Matthew was disturbed by Julius' mood and wondered why Julius would not speak to him. Nevertheless, he would not leave him.

"You have to speak to me, Julius," Matthew mumbled.

"Save for your wife, Mercy, who else will you open up to if not me?" Matthew said gently like he was forcing his words out.

The sight of two frogs chasing an insect caught his attention. He swirled his head and stared.

The insect seemed weak and hopeless already. He looked away as one of the frogs pounced on the insect, his face bearing a grimace.

Matthew jerked himself up as Julius raised his head off his hands and stared into a distant space. For about two minutes Julius continued gazing at nothing, but in a meditating manner. He abruptly stood and slowly turned round a circle, his eyes still wandering into the distance, his lips pursed while not giving the slightest attention to Matthew standing right by him.

Matthew, in clear disquiet for Julius' actions, inquired again if Julius would open up to him. Julius smiled, pursing his lips and turned swiftly so he could stare fully into the empty sky, beholding what he alone could see. He uttered in a loud voice while gesturing with his hand to unseen figures:

"Come! Come! Come, you worthy sons and daughters of Africa, the blessed ones, the demigods that will be respected by the seraphs and the cherubs. Come and place Africa in a path of honour and on its rightful place in the comity of nations. Come, oh you pa-triots!"

His wife's voice over the fence interrupted his trance-like state, beckoning him to come over the house for his meal but he ignored her and continued unabated. He exploded in a deafening shriek, calling out to imaginable people he alone could see.

Julius was obviously not normal, Matthew thought.

Mercy, Julius' wife was dark skinned and in love with her natural black complexion. She spoke against bleaching and lightening and criticized ladies that bleached. She thought it was another form of mental slavery; the constant desire to emulate the white man, their colour and their hair.

All was madness, she believed.

Nothing fitted like her African body and she had a way of making her dark skin glow attractively. She was in all a beautiful woman, with a body so shapely and an angelic face that could be compared to none. Julius was proud of his wife and never failed to boast to his friends that she was the most beautiful and graceful woman God ever gave breath to.

Watching the drama, Matthew lost patience and shook Julius out of his trance, notifying him of his wife's call for lunch. Matthew objected in an incohesive murmur when Julius told him he had food to eat; food that Matthew had no idea of.

"What food is that? Matthew demanded.

"It is the desire to see patriotism sweep all over Africa. That is my delicious food for now," he said and attempted turning another circle. He could not. Something in his mind barred him.

"Is that what is troubling you, Julius?"

Julius nodded. "It's my food, my drink," he said.

"Patriotism; patriotism; yes, patriotism," Matthew mumbled meditatively, his right hand supporting his chin, and nodding gently.

"Patriotism was the food and the drink of our founding fathers, the African founding fathers," Julius continued.

"I am getting you," Matthew responded.

"I have read their histories. In Nigeria we had the likes of Samuel Ajayi Crowther, Tafawa Balewa, Nnamdi Azikiwe, Ahmadu Bello and Obafemi Awolowo. In Ghana, we had the likes of Joseph Danquah and Kwame Nkrumah. In Kenya, we had the likes of Jomo Kenyatta, the Kikuyu nationalist leader, and Tom Mboya. In South Africa, we had the likes of Alfred Xuma, Nelson Mandela, Oliver Tambo, Walter Sisulu, Miriam Makeba and Desmond Tutu," Julius enumerated.

"In the then Republic of the Congo (now the Democratic Republic of the Congo) we had Joseph Kasavubu and Patrice Lumumba as some of their founding fathers," Matthew contributed. "It is assumed that Patrice Lumumba was assassinated for political reasons. Let me stop like this on this sad issue of the assassination. It was an unfortunate incidence for that country and Africa in general."

"Yes, you are correct. In Ethiopia we had Haile Selassie as one of the founding fathers of the nation. Addis Ababa, its capital, means *'new flower'* in Amharic. May Africa be 'flowers' to be admired by all races of the earth," he prayed.

"In Tanzania (the Federation of the Mainland Tanganyika and the island of Zanzibar), we had the likes of Julius Nyerere," Matthew continued.

"There is a meeting point between Nyerere and Mandela,'' Julius interrupted.

"Is it the relinquishing of power by them voluntarily you are talking about?" Matthew asked.

"Yes! I am happy you know that. They were patriots, indeed. Dar es Salaam, the capital of Tanzania, means *'the home of peace.'* When justice reigns, there will be peace in Africa; leaders will do justice; a time is coming when the era of bad governance will be over."

"In Zimbabwe, we have Robert Mugabe; and we had Kenneth Kaunda in Zambia," Matthew continued.

"Yes."

"There were many of them."

"There were many of them, indeed! Other African countries had their own founding fathers too,'' Julius agreed.

"They were visionary leaders with a great dream for the greatness of Africa."

"Call them patriots!"

"Yes, they were. Africa is finished! No more patriots! We are finished?" Matthew lamented like the prophets of old did on the rotten state of any nation.

"Matthew, we are not."

"You must have a reason for saying this. Tell me!"

"Look at the distant horizon. Do you see something there? It is beautiful," Julius spoke after a brief silence, pointing his finger to the distant horizon.

"No, I cannot see anything? What is it?"

Julius smiled.

"Yes, I understand why you cannot see what I am seeing."

"Why can't I see?" Matthew asked.

"You can't. It is a vision. It is only given as a consolation to those who heartily love Africa; those who weep day and night for the realization of the neglected and wasted dream of our patriotic founding fathers - the dream to make Africa great in all aspects."

"I am listening," Matthew said.

"That great dream is a means to an end, a glorious end!"

"What is that end?''

"To make Africans walk with dignity, to be admired and respected anywhere in the world."

"How do we achieve this, Julius?"

"Henceforth, stop calling me Julius. Two days ago, I decided to change my name from Julius to Nelson in honour of Nelson Mandela. He was a great patriot, a true and worthy son of Africa."

"Is that so?"

"Yes, it is. I love him."

"So, how do we Africans go about achieving this great dream of our founding fathers, Julius? Sorry, I meant to say Nelson."

"It is by having leaders and not rulers; leaders that will unselfishly allow the people to jointly enjoy the fountains of the common good." Nelson threw Matthew a searching look, then asked; "Will you become my disciple for patriotism?"

"Ah, Julius," Matthew faltered but would have no objection as long as Nelson's request didn't come with terms. He corrected himself immediately he realized that he just called his friend by his birth name "Julius" instead of "Nelson".

"I can see that you are having difficulties remembering that I am now Nelson. You must not call me Julius, again. Nelson Mandela's patriotic spirit is now in me," Nelson reacted.

"I am still sorry, Nelson."

"That is okay. My terms are always relevant, you know. You haven't answered me. Will you become my disciple on patriotism?"

"*A disciple on patriotism, a disciple on patriotism*," Matthew thought and nodded in assent.

"You must deny yourself and be ready for service," and he quoted these words of M. K Gandhi. '*A patriot cannot afford to ignore any branch of service to the motherland*."[1]

"Anyway, what did you see at the distant horizon?"

"It is a beautiful scene, so beautiful and lovely to behold?"

"Go straight to the point, Nelson?"

"Matthew, how I wish you will be given this vision."

"Stop all this and tell me, please?" Matthew was now anxious.

"Now listen; I hope you will be consoled with this if you truly love Africa, our continent."

"You know I do."

"No, you have not loved it to the point of wanting to die for it."

"It is not you that will tell me this, Nelson. You know I do."

"No, you have not attained the patriotic level. Your love for Africa is still sullied with selfishness. That is why you are not given this vision yet."

"I don't understand you, Nelson," Matthew said.

"Matthew," Nelson called after another brief silence, "I can see in the distant horizon a glow of patriotic Africans rising. They will manifest to bring healing to Africa by eradicating the social, economic and political ills that are ravaging Africa without harm to anyone."

"That is good news."

"Yes, it is. They will lead Africa to achieve great heights in all fronts of human development."

***

Mercy re-appeared and interrupted their discussion, reminding Nelson that his food was getting cold.

***

"This woman does not know that the joy of this wonderful vision is more than the physical food she is so concerned about."

Matthew implored Nelson to answer his wife.

Nelson told her to have no fears for he would soon go and eat.

"She will be happy now," Matthew said.

"Yes, she will. She is well cultured. She has made a home for me."

"A home?"

"Yes, there is a difference between a house and a home."

"Explain, please."

"A home is a house where love and peace reign."

"And a house?"

"Matthew, learn to listen. '*Listen! Or your tongue will make you deaf.*' This is a Cherokee saying," Nelson advised and continued. "Any house without love and peace is not a home. Do you get it?"

"I think so."

"Be emphatic."

"I do."

"Yes, a home is where people are eager to return to from wherever they have gone to. People are afraid to return to a house which is not a home."

"Yes! It is so," Matthew agreed.

"Africa must be made a home for every African. It must be a place for all Africans to love to be; for other races to love to be; and a place where Africans in Diaspora will love to return to with joy and great hopes," Nelson continued.

Matthew reminded Nelson of the migrant tragedy of October (2013) off the Italian island of Lampedusa, in which over 400 African migrants died when unseaworthy vessels carrying them across the Mediterranean Sea to Europe sank. He hoped it doesn't happen again.

"The perished migrants were running away from Africa, their ancestral continent, for greener pastures in Europe. This tragedy will continue to recur unless Africa is made great," Nelson explained.

He shook his head and sighed heavily. He was only short of shedding tears as he realized the enormous potentials in Africa that can make it great but are lying fallow.

"Africa has everything to be like Europe to make her people want to stay here," Matthew observed.

"Yes, Africa has natural resources in abundance. It must be made great and a home for all to stay. Africa has to become a continent that doesn't make Africans to run to other continents for subsistence wages with the attendant embarrassment," Nelson lamented.

"What will be the attributes of these rising patriots?" Matthew asked.

"Let me just tell you a few. They will not love the temporal things of this world but humanity. They will rise above selfishness and greed. They will not be dinosaurs in holding unto power. They will be like Nelson Mandela who willingly handed over power."

"And what again?" Matthew demanded.

"They will abhor foreign aids for they will know that there is nothing that is absolutely free."

"Continue."

"They will be men of honour in the real sense of it."

"These are attributes that will make the economy of Africa to boom and make Africa an attractive business destination for all races of the earth," Matthew said with joy.

"Yes."

"That will be a glorious period in the lives of Africans."

"No doubt about it."

"May God bring this to pass," Matthew prayed.

"He is gracious; He will."

"During that period, Heads of government of Africa will unite to unfasten the shackles of neo-colonialism," Matthew continued.

"You know Kwame Nkrumah promoted Pan-Africanism so as to form a gigantic political machine for Africa. This was not achieved. The rising patriots may not be pre-occupied with this. But one thing is sure; they will seek, without hatred of anyone or country or continent, to liberate Africa from neo-colonialism and all forms of evils."

"So, Nkrumah was a promoter of pan-Africanism?"

"Yes, he was. He actually wanted African independent states to come together to form the United States of Africa but this was not to be. However, he helped in the formation of the Organization for African Unity (OAU) which is now African Union (AU)."

"He was a patriot, indeed."

"He was. That is why he lives on."

"Nkrumah died since 1972! How can you say he lives?"

"Hear what Thomas Campbell said on this. '*To live in hearts we leave behind is not to die.*' Do you understand?"

"I can now understand you."

"Matthew, Nkrumah was great. He saw the dangers of neo-colonialism."

"How?"

"He wrote a book on that titled: *Neo-Colonialism: The Last Stage of Imperialism* (1965). Neo-colonialism has made a mockery of African Independence."

"I wish I could have that book," Matthew said.

"All what true sons and daughters of Africa want is to relate with other people of the world at equal footing for mutual benefits under the sanctity of the Golden Rule which says we should do to others what we want them to do to us."

"Other continents should not be completely blamed for our problems," Matthew said.

"No doubt about that. Africans also have faults. Africans must rise to free our souls from selfishness, greed and inferiority complex. Basically, we have the same human anatomy and blood all over the world. We must be transformed for good."

"Selfishness must give way for the survival and progress of Africa. This cancer must go."

"Matthew, when the rising patriots manifest, they will put an end to this rubbish. They will come. For now, let us prepare for their arrival," Nelson said, ready to take his leave.

Matthew stayed a while after Nelson left for home to watch frogs and toads jump in and out of the pond. A white duck, the only male from appearance, and some black ones, were swimming in the pond. In the sky, an eagle glided slowly, hoping to see a prey.

That is how unpatriotic people are looking for opportunities to cause havoc, especially economic havoc in any nation.

In about ten minutes time, Matthew departed only stopping to stare at the horizon, hoping to catch a glow of the rising patriots but to no avail. He seized his ineffective longing when he remembered that Nelson told him that it was a vision that was only open to true lovers of Africa. '*May be one day the heavens would open for me*', he consoled himself while he trekked on the lonely path down home. For now, he could only hope.

TWO

Behind his compound, Nelson erected a hut for relaxation. It was a thatched roof of grass propped by wooden poles which were cut from the forest at the fringes of Pa. They had a natural resistance to termites and other herbivorous insects. The villagers were familiar with the trees for they had been using them for quite a while. They were of three types and they constituted the largest in the forest for they replenished themselves.

In the hut, Nelson had some modern plastic chairs which were located at the four angles in the hut. Two were whites, the others green. He saw it as an evidence of being patriotic, for the colours represent the Nigerian flag. He wished other Africans would do same with the colours of their flags too. He wouldn't do away with a touch of nature, too. To the West of the hut laid a three-metre mahogany plank. It rested on three pieces of green granite gotten from Saminaka area of Kaduna State, one at each end of it and, the third at its centre to give it balance. The plank was striped alternatively with the Nigerian national colours. Hanging behind this plank, was a laminated copy of the Nigerian National Anthem, glued to a cardboard. During important occasions, the national anthem would be sung in the hut.

On a high table stood a miniature national flag; the bigger one was hung outside above the roof of the hut, hoisted on a steel pole that was mounted on a concrete platform just by the entrance to the hut; a perfect picture of Nelson's national patriotism.

It was in this hut that Mercy placed Nelson's lunch. A typical African dish served in earthen moulds— what was called *Ihen* in koro language. His drink was in a calabash, *Ikwui;Isi-sogh,*the spoon, was a wooden one inherited from his father. He cherished this property for it was no longer in circulation. There was a time his wife misplaced it and it almost triggered a quarrel between them. Since then, everyone in his house knew too well to play with it.

While he ate his lunch, his wife entered the hut and sat beside him.

"Mine, these days you seem different from the man I used to know," she said, her head drooping to the floor.

"What have you noticed?" he mumbled as he swallowed his food.

"You look worried these days. You speak little and you are always staring into the sky. Sometimes you even smile furtively at the sky. Today, you sat at the pond alone, looking into the sky. I was watching you before Matthew came to you. What is the problem? You must tell me," she demanded, her face collapsing in pain.

"I am thinking about the ultimate freedom of Africa, our beloved continent," he said.

"I can now understand. Two weeks ago, I heard you saying these words in a dream.

'Africa, Africa, Africa, the continent endowed with many, diverse and abundant natural resources and with an excellent human capital, a time is coming when patriots in the caste of our founding fathers will walk across your length and breadth to remove shame

from you and….' I shook you out of sleep immediately."

"I cannot remember this," Nelson wondered.

"That is the product of the dominant thought in your mind."

"Mine, one cannot grow beyond his thoughts. Benjamin Disraeli said, *'Nurture your mind with great thoughts for you will never go any higher than you think.*"[1]

"I completely agree with him. We, Africans, must nurture our hearts with great thoughts so as to go higher,"Mercy agreed.

"So, I have been thinking about the greatness of Africa, the natural jewel of the world which is still underdeveloped."

"I can now understand why you have changed recently. Oh, yes."

"Mine, I have changed my name from Julius to Nelson. You are no longer Mrs. Julius Mamman but Mrs. Nelson Mamman," he said after a brief silence.

Mercy demanded the reason for such step.

His teeth exposed in a grin, he asked, "Do you know Nelson Mandela?"

"Yes, I do. It's a global name. In fact, it is a global brand. He is dead."

"That is the man I love to be like. He loved his country, South Africa, and our continent, Africa, so much that he lived in prison for twenty-seven years, refusing conditional freedom by the apartheid regime."

"He was a patriot, indeed."

"Of the first order," Nelson rated. His ear itched. While he was scratching it, a bird flew into the hut. He almost caught it but it flew out to the open windy sky.

"Mine, this is bad omen. What evil is coming to us?" Mercy worried.

"Are you talking about the entry of this bird?"

"Yes!"

"You still believe in superstition?"

"Oh, yes!"

"Come on, no evil will befall this home. That is nonsense. Superstition enslaves. Africans must rise above this."

"I don't know," Mercy remarked.

"Mine, Nelson Mandela had great thoughts concerning the greatness of Africa. As an individual, he walked tall among the giants of this world. He was hoping to see Africa walking tall among the other continents of the world but he has gone home. This could not happen in his life time."

"And so what will you do?"

"I will work for patriotism to reign in Africa. I want to be like him. That is why I decided to change my name from Julius to Nelson."

"But Nelson Mamman is not Nelson Mandela. There is a difference here, Mine."

"You don't want me to change my surname from Mamman to Mandela; do you?"

"Yes, that way you'll change your names totally."

"That will amount to denying my biological father. That is not good."

"I am just teasing you."

"I thought so."

"You see, though names have some degree of influence on the personality of the bearers, what is important is change in attitude," Mercy posited.

"That is true. Williams James said, *'The greatest discovery of my generation is that human beings can alter their lives by altering their attitudes of mind.'*[2]That is what we Africans need. We have the potentials of everything needed to make this continent great."

Mercy nodded.

"We need to clearly carve out the image we want of Africa and sincerely work towards it," Nelson continued.

"There is no doubt Africans have carved out the image we want Africa to be. We only need to sincerely work at achieving it," Mercy said.

"How?" Nelson inquired.

"The good policies of the governments on papers; they speak volumes of the projected image of Africa."

"That is true, Mine."

"Change of attitude; change of attitude is what we need," Mercy continued.

"We need to uphold the law of service, Mine."

"You have gotten it all, Mine," Mercy agreed.

"That I know very well."

"Yes, you do."

"Hear James Allen. *'Only the work that is impersonal can live; the works of self are both powerless and perishable. Where duties, however humble, are done without self-interest and with joyful sacrifice, there is true service and enduring work. Where deeds, however brilliant and apparently successful, are done from love of self, there is ignorance of the law of service and the work perishes.*

"'It is given to the world to learn one great and divine lesson, the lesson of absolute unselfishness. The saints, sages and saviors of all time are they who

have submitted themselves to this task and have learned and lived it."[3]

Mercy was amused by her husband's brilliance; she looked at him and felt her heart skip in joy.

"We must be selfless in the service of our continent to save it from ridicule by international community. That will come to pass when the generation of rising African patriots emerges. I have been given a vision on that," Nelson said with finality.

"See, Matthew, your friend," Mercy gestured towards the approaching mass Matthew ran into. "He walks swiftly! Something might be wrong!" The mass turned to a different direction while Matthew kept on heading to the Nelsons.

"We will hear from him. Let him come."

"Nelson Mandela! Sorry, Nelson Mamman! My Son, Paul, has come back from school!" Matthew began.

"What is the matter?" Nelson asked.

"He told me that his teacher admonished the students to be patriotic Africans."

"Continue."

"My son said the teacher spoke passionately about making Africa great. That they were moved in their hearts and have resolved to be patriotic Africans in order to make the continent great."

"What did he say again?"

"He said he has changed his name like you!"

"To what name?"

"To Africana! That it will always remind him to be patriotic. You have gotten a disciple!"

Nelson smiled, his eyes glowing with hope. He raised his head and looked at the distant horizon, smiled again, and lowered it.

"What is it again, Nelson?"

"Africana, your son, could be one of the rising patriots I have seen in the horizon. They will be all over Africa. They will come to lead, not to rule, the people with justice. They will walk their talk. May God allow my eyes to see these beautiful *flowers* that will adorn Africa, our continent."

"That is the reason behind my rushing here," Matthew said.

"But will they be patriotic to remove the shame from Africa?" Mercy asked.

"They will. It has been ordained by the heavens. They will truly love Africa. That is why I have been shown the vision," Nelson replied.

"Yes, there is nothing that can stand against true love," Matthew said.

"That is true," Nelson agreed.

"The patriots will have pure love for Africa."

"Yes, they will, Matthew," Nelson said.

"They will then be indomitable patriots,"Matthew remarked, bending down to scratch his leg.

A black insect was biting him. He squeezed it and the blood spluttered on his hands. He looked with disgust and then cleaned his hands with a dirty piece of cloth he picked from the ground. He washed the hands with lather after that.

"Exactly! No one will destroy them," Nelson exclaimed.

"May we live to see those glorious days," Mercy prayed.

***

Nelson Mamman's compound had three buildings; each building had three rooms. One of the buildings sat on the left of the entrance to the housewhile the other, on the right, directly opposite it. The third building faced the entrance to the house and about twenty metres away from it. Behind it was a garden of oranges, mangoes, guavas and grapes. Some flowers like queen of the night, hibiscus, flamboyant, and pride of Barbados perched within the garden, enhancing its beauty. It made the heart tingled with joy seeing sparrows perched from one branch to another before gliding into their nests on some trees in the garden. The garden was generally a lovely place to be. The family used it for recreational activities. On this fateful day, Nelson Mamman, his wife, Mercy, and Matthew strolled casually into the garden to relax.

***

Matthew appreciated the garden for it soothed his soul anytime he sat in there

Mercy noticed how bright and peaceful he was and it delighted her.

"So you love this garden?" Mercy asked.

"I sincerely do. It is a nice place to be."

"Matthew," Mercy called, "life is all about living to please God. That is its essence."

"That is right. To be merciful and serve others in justice pleases God. That is true worship," Matthew agreed.

While Mercy and Matthew were talking, Nelson was silent, thinking deeply. After some minutes, he rose up with a smile and turned a circle like he had done before and silently beckoned the rising African patriots from the four corners of the world to come.

"Matthew, my husband is sick! Look what he is doing! Why?" Mercy cried in dismay.

"Oh you patriots, the hope of Africa, the continent of the blacks, come and save us. Come from Brazil, the Caribbean islands, Europe, the Arab world, America... and within Africa soil to build Africa," Nelson said, turning in a circle again, making Mercy more worried.

"What has become of my husband?" she asked. "Is it madness?"

"Madam, relax. He is not mad. He is excited by the vision of the rising African patriots he sees in the horizon."

"He is also mentioning places beyond Africa," Mercy said in surprise.

"Brazil, the Caribbean islands, Europe, the Arab world and America he mentioned?" Matthew asked, laughing.

"Yes!"

"Yes, these are places that many able-bodied and productive Africans were taken to as slaves since the 15th Century. Some of the rising African patriots are also the descendants of these slaves. They are our people; our blood."

"And they will come to develop Africa?"

"Yes, they will come. It is a vision from God."

"Matthew, they are no longer thinking, speaking and acting like Africans. They called our children schooling in overseas countries African boys while seeing themselves as non-Africans. They have been absorbed into the white man's culture in all aspects of life."

"No matter what, an African is still an African. He knows and feels it. He cannot deny that," he said while staring at two birds courting each other in the sky. He wished a time would come when Africa would be courted by other continents like that.

"Matthew, the epoch of slavery covered a period of more than four centuries (1445 – 1870). It was about 426 years; that was a long time."

"And so what are you trying to say?"

"These black people that are still in the white man's land will not like to come back."

"The Israelites stayed in Egypt for over 430 years! There is a surprising coincidence here. The Africans were enslaved for about 426 years, almost the same number of years the Israelites stayed in Egypt."

"What are you trying to say again?" Mercy asked.

"Were the Israelites not liberated to develop Israel to where it is today? So shall Africa be. Many Africans in Diaspora have come to trace their roots."

"But the Africans are no longer physically enslaved?"

"Yes, you are right. But we are presently enslaved mentally. We must be liberated from this!"

"That is right. This, I know," Mercy agreed.

"Yes, both the Africans in the continent and in Diaspora must be liberated from mental and unhealthy attitudinal enslavement. We must throw off the chains, the fetters and the shackles that entangle us mentally for total freedom," Matthew continued.

"So, even Africans in Diaspora will love to come back to Africa?" Mercy asked.

"Yes, the rising African patriots even in Diaspora will come home to develop Africa," Matthew said.

"May it come to pass in our days," Mercy prayed.

"By the grace of God," Matthew remarked.

Nelson started chanting a song in his native language, *Koro*. The song is titled *Inom Irishiya Igbani* (Good Days Are Coming).

The song was about the rising African patriots that would place Africa upon the commanding height of dignity. The tone of the song was pitiful and emotional like songs of the black South Africans during their struggle for freedom against apartheid. It was also similar to slave songs that the ancestors of African-Americans sang while working in plantations during slavery. It also had the tone of freedom songs by African Americans during the days of the Civil Rights Movement when the sit-ins, the swim-ins and the matches were staged, and during which time the great Martin Luther King Jr. was assassinated. This made him emotional and his eyes welled with tears.

Matthew had always been a man who controlled his emotions, but this time, he failed. He could not withstand the emotions the songs sparked in him. He joined Nelson who was already dancing and they sang and danced together. Nelson wondered why the stories of the agonies the slaves were subjected to could not inspire Africa to rise and emancipate the continent from its deplorable state of underdevelopment— to be as glorious as other continents. The lyrics go:

Africa (2x), our great continent!
You shall be liberated from the African and non-African hawks.
It is no longer the non-Africans only that hinder your progress.
Many of your sons and daughters are also involved because of lack of patriotism.

But rejoice, the lovely black lady.
In no distant future, you will give birth to patriotic children because you are already pregnant with them.
They will walk all over you with dignity.
No longer will you be ridiculed.
They will stand in dignity with any
Other worlds.
They will resist vain glory.
They will make good use of your abundant natural resources for the good of all.
They will make your name great.
No longer will the world associate your name with hunger, diseases, selfishness, greed and under-development.
From the four corners of the world, people will come to see your glorious beauty and marvel.
Oh Africa! Africa, my mother, I love you.

"Matthew, are you also mad?" Mercy asked.

"I am not. You won't understand. Just watch us," he continued to dance.

***

While Nelson and Matthew were singing and dancing, Nelson's uncle came to the garden. Anytime he visited, he preferred sitting in the garden because it was more refreshing. He listened to the song and shook his head in sorrow as he remembered the stories of the cries of the Africans whose productive sons and daughters were sold into slavery in exchange for items of luxury and minimal economic fortunes by African rulers to work in the plantations of the West. This was one of the primary factors Walter Rodney, a South African writer, said led to the present underdevelopment of Africa.

"Julius, you are singing a song about the greatness of Africa to come. Can this be possible?"

"Uncle, it is possible," Nelson responded.

"I am afraid."

"Why, uncle?"

"Most of us, Africans are driven by different interests unlike Europeans. We are so selfish, heedless of common good."

"Uncle, I see a new breed of African patriots in the horizon. They will come to make Africa great."

"May that come to be."

"That is what I want to hear from you, uncle. Thank you."

"My daughter," uncle gestured towards Mercy, "how are you doing?" he asked.

"I am doing fine, uncle. You are much welcome."

"Thank you."

"Uncle, I have been thinking of seeing you," Mercy said.

"Me? Hope all is fine?"

"My husband acts strange lately. I think he is sick."

"Mine, stop that. I am well. I am only excited by the vision of the rising African patriots in the horizon. The vision gives me joy," Nelson interrupted.

"My daughter, relax. There is nothing wrong with him," the uncle advised.

"Nelson," Matthew called, "I am going home. We will see later."

"Are you now called Nelson?" the uncle asked.

"Yes, uncle; I want to be like Nelson Mandela. I will sacrifice my energy, time, money, materials and my life, if it warrants making Africa great again." He was not reserved. It is now a mission in his life.

"From the passion I am seeing in you, Africa shall be great; indeed, if other Africans will be passionate about its greatness as you are."

"Yes, thank you uncle, just wait and see," Nelson maintained.

THREE

ꕥ

It was a restless night for Nelson. He was sleeping on a bamboo bed with only a lion skin as bed-sheet. His grandfather, who was a hunter, had killed many dangerous animals including lions when he was alive. Therefore, the family had many lion skins. It was a tradition in their family not to sell lion skins. They only used them and occasionally gave them out as presents to important visitors. To them, important visitors were patriotic people who had shown courage in the face of any type of danger. A lion's skin given as a present from the Mammans was highly revered. Many people knew this.

Nelson Mamman slept on the bamboo bed to deny himself good sleep so as to keep awake to think over the state of the continent, the African continent, throughout the night and to chart a way forward for its development. But why sleep on a lion's skin? Because he wanted Africans to live, think, speak and act like the lion, the animal that conquers and dominates its environment, the animal that is fearless and walks with dignity. He remembered the story about the lions that inhabited the surrounding forests in the village and how they would periodically sneak into peoples' homes and prey on their goats.

He had also been told of how a man called Negwe Ukuangh, a fearless man with great knowledge of medicinal herbs, went after a lioness one day with only but an axe and wrestled a goat from it alive. The lioness had caught the only goat of a man called Mami.

Mami was a poor man. Negwe Ukuangh had pity on him and decided to show this act of bravery that led to saving the goat and killing the lioness. Nelson believed that Africans should be brave to redeem the lost glory of Africa from unpatriotic people. Nelson craved for the earlier civilization that boomed in Africa before the coming of the Europeans.

His mind kept wandering through the night and the night never seemed to get bright. It was like eternity to Nelson, his eyes wide open looking at nothing. He went out many times and stared at the stars, shining in their full glory. He wished Africans would arise and shine likewise, first in Africa and then all over the world, to bring honor to Africa by restoring her lost glory.

History had it that Africa's development was arrested by the evil of slavery. I am not a historian but the historians would always insist that this piece of history was a fact.

Oh, no! I cannot go further on this. It is so disgusting. However, it must be convincing, and it is, that Africa was not sleeping at the rudimentary stage of universal development or the conquest of nature to enhance the quality of life through qualitative and massive production as Walter Rodney would argue.

Yes, it was said that the smelting of iron ores for improved implements of production before the 15th century contact with any other continental civilization supports this. But there should be no hatred over this. Africans must remember the reconciliatory spirit of the late Madiba, Nelson Mandela, with the racists in South Africa and follow his step to forge ahead. The winds of hatred must not blow away the footprints of love Madiba left in the sand of time.

"You patriots, rising in the horizon, will one day unselfishly shine all over Africa like these stars that are generously illuminating the earth now. You patriots will be unselfish like these stars and you will put away the canker worm of selfishness which has caused the darkness that pervades Africa. Yes, Africa, the garments of global scorn will be removed from you. You shall be the toast of the world," Nelson thought as he gazed at the starry sky, dazzling with the brightness of the stars.

There were no clouds on that night to interfere with the beauty and the brightness of the stars. It was a silent night that presented a scene as if all the inhabitants of the earth were keeping deadly silence before a passing god that was void of mercy. Only the shrieks of nocturnal insects that periodically punctured this silence could be heard. So it was a memorable silence which he would never forget.

Nelson returned to the room and stretched himself on the bamboo bed. It was not his bed and it didn't fit his frame. For him to be comfortable on the bed, he must lie in a diagonal position. However, he still couldn't sleep. Why would he? He wanted it so. A thought flashed his mind to sensitize his students on patriotism during his history class in the morning. He was determined to see to the grooming of an army of African patriots. God was doing that already.

***

Wednesday morning, Nelson was in school by 7.00 am. The school had been in existence for twenty-seven years. Many trees that were planted by patriotic Nigerians at the inception of the school had grown to admirable heights, forming formidable breakers against violent storms and casting thick shadows. It was a tempting site for relaxation because of the cool environment. Nelson sat under one of those trees, waiting for Kweku, the cleaner, to finish sweeping the staff room. As he waited, he flipped through pages of a biography book of some African founding fathers. The staff room was a spacious hall with tables and chairs for every teacher. Kweku approached Nelson under the shades to inform him that the staff room was set.

"Kweku, you are a patriot," Nelson said, his eyes fixed on him.

Kweku hailed from Accra in the Greater Accra Region in Ghana. He came to Nigeria with his uncle many years ago. He heard so much about the patriotic acts of past African founding fathers and had been baptized into patriotism since then. That spirit remained in him as he visited Ghana every two years. He owned a house that sat on a slope in the western part of Accra. His first son, Appiah, whom he had trained in Europe to be an engineer and now an asset to Ghana, built the house for him.

Appiah was patriotic enough to return to Ghana after his studies in Europe so as to help in the development of his country. Kweku had refused to return to Ghana even with the progress he had made in life. He was humble enough to carry on as a cleaner. Nelson wished every African would be like Kweku; be an asset and not a liability to Africa.

"Why, sir?" Kweku demanded to know why Nelson said he was a patriot.

"I have been in this school for the past three years. You have never been late to the school. You always come early to get the office ready for us, the teaching staff. That is patriotism."

"Sir, I have heard about the patriotism of our founding fathers. They wanted Africa to be great. I must not fail them by being unpatriotic. This, their noble dream, must be realized."

"If every African will think and be like you, in no distant future, Africa shall be the darling of the world," Nelson said.

"Sir, the whole thing is disturbing. For example, many teachers, in this school, are not like you. They come to school late and close early. They are setting bad examples for the young ones. How will Africa be great with this kind of attitude?" Kweku lamented.

"That is one of the problems with us in most establishments," Nelson agreed.

"Sir, these days," Kweku resumed, "I have been observing you under that tree," Kweku pointed at the tree.

"You are always sitting and meditating alone, is anything the problem?"

Kweku's face avoided Nelson's stare and drooped to the earth.

"It is what we are talking of right now. The lack of patriotism in all we do. It is burrowing hurt inside me. I desire to see patriotism reigning in Africa."

"I understand."

"Yes, that is what I have been thinking about," Nelson continued.

Kweku looked at Nelson with admiration and said, "Blessed is the womb that bore you. You are a worthy son of Africa. God will grant to you your noble desire."

"Thank you, baba," Nelson responded.

"My son let us pray for the good of Africa. Let us be on our knees," Kweku suggested.

"Oh, Lord, our overall papa in heaven; papa for everybody; everybody in this world; impartial papa who sees everybody and knows our thoughts; thank you for creating Africa; thank you for Africans. Thank you for everything that is African. We thank you for the many and abundant natural resources you have put in our lands. We thank you for the good climate. Oh papa, you have been so good to Africa that other continents wish to have what you have given to us. With sympathy to some other continents, rarely do we experience natural disasters such as tornadoes, earthquakes, wildfires and.... I thank you, papa, for everything. But papa, forgive all of us Africans. We have not patriotically used the resources you have given to us. We have greatly disappointed you and embarrassed ourselves before other continents. We have intentionally and wrongly become dwarfs among them in our thoughts and actions. Though slavery and colonialism greatly contributed to this, we ought not to be at the present stage of low development. Revive us, papa; oh, revive us, papa; I pray, revive us papa so that we will remove the shame from us and make Africa great. Bless Nelson and

grant to us the desires of our hearts, the realization of Africa greatness. Amen."

"Thank you, baba," Nelson said, wiping tears from his face.

"Stop weeping, my son. I have a dream that a time will come when patriotism will come to stay in Africa. When this time comes, the continent of Africa will have an effective voice in international affairs because Africans will be admired and respected by all."

"Baba, you are right. That time will come. Come and see why I agreed with what you have just said," Nelson said, moving away from the shade of the tree. Kweku trailed him.

"What is it, my son?"

"Baba, look over there," he beseeched, pointing his finger to the distant horizon where it seems to unite with a coarse hilltop with dense trees.

"My son, you know I am almost 60 years of age. My eyes are failing me. I can't see well. Okay, let me put on my pair of medicated glasses. They are new. I collected them yesterday from Dr. Arroja. Do you know him?"

"I do. He is also a Ghanaian like you. He is from the Western Region of Ghana. He treated my aged mother last year."

"I see," he said, putting on the pair of the glasses.

"Can you now see what I am seeing?"

"No, Nelson. What is it?"

"It is a glorious view. In that distant horizon, a new generation of African patriots is arising. It is a great multitude from the four corners of the world."

Kweku still looked up, with the palm of his right hand, resting at an appropriate angle on his forehead to enhance his vision, but he still could not see anything. Actually, his eyes were failing him but that was not the reason why he could not see the rising patriots.

"Sorry; it is a vision. You cannot see it until you are given. The tears of every African country shall be wiped away by these coming patriots," Nelson continued.

"By that time I would have gone home."

"Baba, with this knowledge, you will go home in peace."

"Let the name of the LORD be praised!" Kweku exclaimed.

"Baba, will you like when you die to be buried here in Nigeria or in Ghana?" Nelson asked.

"Nelson, Africa is Africa. An African is an African, no matter where he or she comes from. Therefore, it does not matter where one is buried in Africa."

"Baba, I agree with you. May God give all Africans this understanding towards unity?"

"Amen."

"Baba, you once told me that your son was attending an orthopedic hospital because of some leg challenge."

"Yes."

"Who is his doctor?"

"It is Dr. Amoudou, the Senegalese."

"The popular Dr., Sekou Amoudou?"

"Yes. You know he is a patriotic African."

"Tell me about him, baba."

Kweku cleared his throat and advised that they return to the shade of the tree under which they were standing before.

"A story," Kweku began, "was told of how Dr. Amoudou refused to co-operate with a non-African. I don't remember which country the non-African came from." He halted for some seconds.

"Continue, baba," Nelson said, his eyes wide opened and his face bright.

"The non-African wanted Dr. Amoudou to reveal to him a secret that has to do with a unified and strategic plan to develop Africa, the revelation of which would pain Africa to the bone. Dr. Amoudou refused."

"That should be a strategic plan against anti-Africa forces that are militating against Africa's development."

"You have gotten it, my son."

"Dr. Amoudou demonstrated patriotism in this case, baba. I like that."

"The non-African was angry with Dr. Amoudou."

"Why won't he be, baba?"

"Oh, yes! But at last, he commended Dr. Amoudou for his patriotism."

"Oh, what…"

"My son, you may wish to note that Dr. Amoudou is a member of a Think Tank for the Development of Africa [TTDA]," he interrupted.

"I heard you, baba. He displayed courage, baba! Patriotism! Dr. Amoudou is my type of man, any day."

"That is it! The white man will not speak evil of his country. He does not tolerate anybody speaking evil of his country."

"That is what we Africans have failed to understand. We ridicule one another and portray our countries and our continent in bad light," Nelson said.

"The way people in a continent see and conduct themselves will be the way other people will see and treat them," Kweku said.

***

"Nelson! Nelson! Nelson! Matthew's voiced echoed in the compound in a high pitch as he ran towards Nelson who was standing with Kweku under the tree.

"What is the matter?" Nelson asked.

"Ahmad Youssef of Morocco is dead. Another African light has passed on," Matthew reported, looking worried.

Ahmad Youssef had been a strong advocate for patriotism. He believed progress came from upholding African customs and traditions in order to cover the wide gap in development between Africa and other continents. He was always reminding Africans that Africa was in no way lagging behind other continents when rudimental development was evolving universally. He would say that the negative cultures we imbibed from the west area clogged in the wheel of our progress. He was highly supportive of civilized resistance by Africans for any challenge against the progress of Africa. That was his philosophy. Now, he had taken a glorious exit! He was among the few vestiges of African zealots who were desperate for the coming of the future patriots. His exit had created a big vacuum.

Nelson had been reading articles written by late Ahmad Youssef on the lack of patriotism in Africa. He was one of Ahmad Youssef's unacknowledged disciples. Matthew knew that and it was the main reason why he had run to break the sad news of the death to him.

The news of Ahmad Youssef's death was disheartening for Nelson. He lowered his head and sighed heavily. After some minutes he jerked himself on his feet, lifting his hands up to heaven in frustration and questioned God. He asked why African patriots were dying. He questioned if God could see and why he didn't stop the ill fate.

In his confusion, Nelson heard a voice saying, *"Don't be discouraged, Nelson. Be strong and watch the new thing God is about to do in Africa. You have been given just a tip of it in the vision. Have you not? The old patriots are called to rest. They have endured the pains of un-patriotism so much all these while. God is going to cause patriotism to reign in Africa. The rising patriots you have seen in the vision will be His special people and the joy of His heart for they will lead Africans with justice and mercy. He will bring all Africans under one umbrella of unity and patriotism. Be consoled with this. But you will be taken away before their physical manifestation. Therefore, be content with the vision and more of it that will be given to you before you die."*

"Thank you, the blessed one. Thank you, the blessed one. Let the will of the LORD be done in my life for He is perfect in all His ways. Even if I die now, I am satisfied with what He is about to do in Africa. Thank you, Lord, the Great one," Nelson spoke audibly to the amazement of Matthew and Kweku. He understood that it was the still voice of an angel that had spoken to him.

"This," Kweku said, referring to Ahmad Youssef, "was one of the remaining patriots that were preventing the total destruction of the economy of

Africa by unpatriotic Africans. Heaven listens to their supplications day and night for the survival of Africa."

"Who will stand in the gap for God to spare Africans? He is angry because Africans have refused to harness and use the abundant resources bestowed in the continent for development," Matthew asked.

"Ahmad Youssef, Ahmad Youssef, my mentor; though we did not meet physically, you had been my guiding light. Now you are gone. You are gone. You are gone. May your soul rest in peace because African patriots are rising in the horizon to bring to Africa the manifestation of your dream on patriotism. My warm regards to our late founding fathers. Till we come," Nelson lamented.

Nelson looked up the tree and saw a dove that had just perched on one of the branches and said, "You dove, it is said that you symbolize peace. As you perch on this tree, may peace descend on Africa by the coming of the rising patriots."

Matthew picked a stone nearby and was about throwing at the bird when it glided into the air and up it flew into the sky.

"Stop that! This is not the time for hunting birds. It is a time for mourning. Let us mourn the passing on of Ahmad Youssef," Nelson cautioned.

The dove flew over a river, running through a forested area in the west of Pa and perched on a tree rooted in a lateritic hill just about 50 meters away from the bank of the river. It didn't stay there for a long time for it was scared by the sight of an old man with a gun. The man was hunting for antelopes. He would kill no wild animal save for antelopes. That was a standing order in their clan over the centuries. He would not go against it. And how was the dove supposed to know this and perched still on a branch?

Matthew lowered his hand to drop the stone he wanted to stone the dove with. It escaped his hand falling on the foot of Kweku. Kweku shouted like a child and quickly bent down to massage the foot. He pursed his mouth, clenched his teeth and groaned.

"Sorry, baba. I am sorry, please," Matthew apologized.

"You should have been careful when dropping the stone," Nelson said before deciding to head back home.

The death of Ahmad Youssef had devastated Nelson like any other lover of Africa. He was no longer emotionally stable to teach the class. His excitement to sensitize the class on patriotism had been dampened at that moment. This would be done another day and not on this day of continental mourning. He returned to his home in silence without saying a word further. Matthew followed him silently as he walked back home.

Kweku was left alone, watching them go and wondering about the would-be exploits of the coming African patriots.Everybody will agree that it was a pathetic scene .

FOUR

ഇറ

"Mine, what has happened to you, again?" Mercy asked Nelson while they were seated in one of the rooms in their house. She noticed that his countenance was somber. She understood he was sad. The death of Ahmad Youssef had so much emotional effect on him; it showed in his manners.

"He is mourning. I am also mourning," Matthew revealed, looking sad. He turned to look at a black and white photograph of Nelson's late paternal grandfather, Barde, hanging on the wall in the sitting room. It had been darkened by smoke over the years because they usually built fire in the room with dry woods mostly fetched from the hills of Pa to warm the rooms during the cold season, especially in the harmattan. Barde died before Nelson was born. When he was to be photographed, the stories said, he vehemently refused. It was after serious persuasion that he consented grudgingly. He thought the picture would be taken to the white man's land to be used to poke fun at the black man. He was wrong for it was only fair to agree that the white man's ways are not totally bad for some of them are honestly commendable. The photograph was now the only thing that helped Nelson know what his grandfather looked like.

Looking at the prominent forehead in the picture, Nelson couldn't help but agree that he looked like his grandfather. Genetic mysteries— how does a trait transfer from one generation to another? According to oral sources, it was one Mr. Six Thatcher, a heavily built British with thick lips and blue-searching eyes, who took the photograph. He was a senior Forestry Officer in the colonial era.

Mr. Thatcher was in Pa on an official assignment to Gujehi Forest when he made the acquaintance of Pa Barde and eventually snapped a photograph of him to keep memories. Gujehi Forest was the name of the forest in the east of Pa.

"Who has gone again?" Mercy asked, holding her hands, pressed against her chest; her heart was beating fast. She feared it was a relation.

"Ahmad Youssef, a Moroccan," Matthew answered.

"Who was he?" she felt relieved knowing it wasn't any of her relation; though any other death worried her but she was more disturbed if the deceased was a family member or a close friend. She loved people; even those not from Pa knew she did.

"He was an African patriot. He loved Africa wholeheartedly. He was willing to pay the supreme price for that."

Nelson was quiet up to this moment, reminiscing about the scene at the pond when he ignored Matthew for some time, brooding over the demise of Ahmad Youssef.

"I can now understand. Nelson mentioned this name about two months ago while reading one of the dailies," Mercy recalled.

"Yes, he loves the man so much."

"He loved him, not that he loves him. He is dead," Mercy contented.

"No! I am correct. He still loves him even in death. He will ever remember him with loving memories."

"You seem to be right."

"I am."

"While he was calling the name that day, he kissed the photograph of Youssef," Mercy continued to recall.

"He is fond of that whenever he reads the exciting stories of the patriots no matter which continent they belong to."

"Any continent?" Mercy was surprised.

"Yes! Your husband wished that justice should reign all over the world. He loves mankind without racial segregation."

"He has been telling me that."

"He is not only thinking about the African continent. He wants every continent to progress but not at the expense of others," Matthew continued.

"That is a universal man who really fits this era of globalization which ought not to have racial discrimination and especially on economic matters that Africa is trying to make up with the rest of the world. The *Washington Consensus* should take note of this. That is a topic in itself for another day, anyway.

"One day, he confronted a man from one of the countries in Central Africa for calling a patriotic European an idiot, a mad man."

"Where was that?"

"I can't remember but it was during an international conference on good governance. He told me this," Matthew narrated.

"Yes, he travels on sponsorship for international conferences periodially," Mercy said.

"If the people from other continents will look at the world as united like your husband, it will be a better place to live."

"That is true. That day I was surprised at his action. I asked him what that means."

"What did he tell you?"

"He laughed and said to me, *'Mine, you won't understand. The spirit of this man is great. He is one of the few living patriotic Africans, shedding light on our path to ultimate freedom.'*"

"He told me some time ago that late Ahmad Youssef had risen above the enticements of this world that entangles many people," Matthew recalled.

"So, Nelson has been discussing the man with you?"

"Yes. That is why I came to tell him of his death. He had no idea."

"What can I offer you? Tea, coffee or *peteh*?" Mercy asked Matthew.

"*Peteh*, the African dish, but not now."

"The African dish?"

"That is correct! You got me. I must be patriotic even in the choice of dishes."

"That is Matthew on African patriotism!" Mercy exclaimed spiritedly. Why not? Matthew was her husband's close friend and was the best man at their wedding. They had been socially free with each other. This should be so.

"When Africans take pride in what is African, markets will be created for our produce. When our products become popular it means more money for our economy," Matthew explained.

"I agree with you. We must grow our economy. Nobody else will do that for us," Mercy agreed, bending down to get rid of an insect that was biting her ankle.

"Every African must know that. But this does not mean that we should not relate economically with other continents. World economy is a web of national economies."

"You are right, Matthew. But all countries must do that under the concept of mutual benefit, taking the principle of comparative advantage into consideration."

"No country is an economic island. But no nation should survive at the expense of the others. A global economic policy must be aimed at," Matthew said.

"That is right."

"Progressive people all over the world badly desire to see this happen," Matthew continued.

"Matthew, are you so disturbed about Ahmad Youssef's death that you cannot eat?"

"Yes, it is part of it," he murmured.

"Remember the consolation," Mercy reminded.

"What is it?" Matthew could not reason out what she meant.

"The vision; the vision."

"Of the rising African patriots?" he asked, recalling with a mixture of joy and sorrow; joy, for the coming patriots; sorrow, for the death of Ahmad Youssef. He sighed.

"That is it!"

"But we still need pockets of patriotic light here and there to brighten, though feebly, the darkened political and economic firmaments and…"

The flow was interrupted by the sight of a hen that was tending to her chicks. She picked pieces of whole and broken grains, here and there, for the chicks. She would not help herself until they were satisfied. Matthew, now a silent disciple of Nelson, mumbled that the coming patriots would be like the hen. They would be fathers and mothers to all. They would not rest until they saw that Africans were satisfied politically and economically. He knew social satisfaction depended on the achieving of these two, so he left that to be figured out.

"Continue," Mercy said in eagerness.

"And to welcome the rising patriots, the hope of Africa," Matthew concluded, glancing at Nelson, wondering why he was silent.

Nelson inhaled heavily and took a soothing breath. He released pent up emotional stress developed as a result of Ahmad Youssef's death, the great Moroccan patriot. Mercy and Matthew concentrated wholly on him, their eyes bulging out of sockets, looking at him, waiting.and expecting his next move.

Mercy wanted to say something to Nelson, but Matthew prevented her. Nelson stood up and looked towards north-western Africa, the Maghreb, where Morocco lies with its long coast of the Atlantic Ocean that was once a route for slavery. Nelson remembered this. *"The taking of the slaves to Europe reduced the African productive capital. Now, the African patriotic capital has been reduced by the passing on of Ahmad Youssef,"* he silently thought, his eyes welled in tears. He swiped the tears out with the back of his hand before they dropped.

Mercy and Matthew kept on watching Nelson silently, expecting him to turn a full circle as before. This time, it was not going to be so. Nelson knew that modesty was a virtue. He also knew when it was overstayed. He was also intelligent and dramatic enough to keep people in suspense.

Nelson continued to look towards Morocco for quite some time and then he uttered in a loud voice;*'Oh, Morocco, Morocco, you that houses oases of water; from you, this day, Africa has again lost an oasis of patriotism in the person of Ahmad Youssef. But be comforted; let all patriotic African sons and daughters be comforted. Many rivers of patriotism will soon traverse and flood our continent. These are the patriots rising in the horizon. Even if you, Moroccans, stand at Jabel Toubka, the highest peak (4,165metres) of your country, you will not see them unless you are true lovers of Africa. Oh, Africans! It is a vision. Let the hills, the plateaus and the mountains of unpatriotism be leveled, and its valleys be filled, ready for their coming. He that is unpatriotic must straighten his ways. They will not tolerate this. The patriotic rivers will cut across even unpatriotic rocky grounds without resistance. They will remove all clogs that block the progress of Africa.'*

He moved to the garden at the backyard when he finished. Mercy and Matthew followed him silently. The departure of a loved one should be respected and mourned in African culture.

***

While at the garden, Nelson tuned a radio, not having any particular channel in mind but was very fortunate to stumble on a channel that was casting news on the death of Ahmad Youssef in this manner:

"Ahmad Youssef of Morocco is dead. The world renowned Moroccan was known, admired and respected for his principled stance on patriotism for the continent without hatred towards the West for the offences of slavery and colonialism which some people said retarded the development of Africa as believed by many. He lived, advocating with passion for Africans to imbibe the culture of patriotism in all they think, speak and do. He rightly believed, with the spirit of patriotism, Africans can close the gap in industrial development that now temporarily exists between Africa and the other continents. He tenaciously held to this view until his death. He has since been buried.

"The best tribute to be given to this late and worthy son of Africa, who was admired and respected even by racial whites, is for Africans to pick up the broom of patriotism and sweep away all forms of political and economic indecency that have prevented the progress of Africa and bring all Africans under one political and economic umbrella. That is the tribute that will make the spirit of this great, even in death, Ahmad Youssef, to rest in peace and not flowery and empty words that are void of the spirit of patriotism,"

The news caster was short of saying that it was the spirit of the words that mattered and not the letters.

"Ahmad Youssef, good bye, good bye. I wish I was in Morocco when your remains were received by mother earth," Nelson lamented, switching off the radio. He would not listen to any other news for the day apart from that of his hero, the late Youssef.

***

Mercy glanced up and saw on the tree over them a green mamba, an African tropical snake, waiting in ambush for a potential prey, a squirrel. Mercy even saw where the snake hid in uncaring abandon before the squirrel approached. The squirrel had no idea what evil awaited it, but it was spared its death.

"Mine! Matthew! Run! Run!" Mercy shouted, her hands flapping loosely in the air, her voice loud and vibrating; unsettling the birds perching peacefully on the trees in the garden.

Nelson turned towards her, inquiring what the outburst was for. He tried to stay composed but was actually struggling to control the fear pent up on his brow, sending jitters down his spine. Fear was effeminate and for weaker men.

For real men, emotional control in all circumstances was the norm. Yes, real men; not all men though. The real men are always calm even in the worst of circumstances, thinking clearly on how to act accordingly. They do turn obstacles to bicycles to ride themselves to achieve great heights in life.

"A snake!"

"Where is it?"

"On that tree!" she said, pointing at its direction on the tree but it was nowhere there anymore. Like the birds, the snake was scared by Mercy's sharp voice. It swiftly glided out of sight.

A green snake, it blended easily with the green leaves. It must have hidden inside one of the tree's darkest corners.

"Mine, you didn't see any snake, did you?" Nelson demanded.

"Don't tell me that! I am serious! It is a green snake," she insisted, her eye fixed on the position she saw it. She noticed leaves shake on a twig; then the snake's head extending out of the leaves to survey the environment whether it was safe for escape. The snake felt the pressure from a body and quickly writhed inward.

"See it there, in that branch!" Mercy shouted, pointing at the branch. The green mamba heard the shout, and felt it was no longer safe. In the blink of an eye it disappeared again. It hurt Mercy that Nelson and Matthew would think her paranoid or untruthful for they had at no point in time saw the snake. She knew Nelson would still insist that she did not see a snake and would continue to tease her.

Ishinin? What? Could he do that in that period of mourning? No! Nelson would spare her because of that. He wouldn't be in the mood to tease her. Not when a patriot had just died.

And thus the squirrel was saved from unperceived danger, not knowing how lucky it had been.

"Green mamba is very dangerous," Matthew agreed. Tete-Susami, his late uncle, told him when he was a child. He was close to him. He told him many African folk tales which were the norms back then. The culture of telling folk tales was now extinct in Africa.

Oh, I wish that it may be revived to instill moral and patriotic lessons into the young ones.

"I have heard that, too, Matthew. It is very dangerous," Nelson said, still looking at the tree, imagining whether it was actually a snake Mercy saw.

"Let us move away from this garden," Mercy suggested, tending to move in fear of snakes. "*Some might still be there,*" she thought.

"To where?" Nelson asked.

"To the house!" she replied.

"That is not the solution. What we need to do is to keep snakes away from this garden by keeping it neat. This is the first time a snake is said to be seen here. Did you actually see it?" Nelson still doubted.

She sighed in frustration. It hurt being doubted on a reality that however had no prove. She could not bring back the snake as a proof. How she wished it would be possible.

"The garden is full of weeds," Nelson continued. "I wanted to clear it sometime last week. Something prevented me. Headache! I remember," He contorted his face as if the headache returned as soon as it was mentioned.

"With the noise, if it was actually a snake, it might have run far away from there," Matthew said, pretending not to be afraid. It was wrong and shameful to do that in the presence of a woman. But he did. Mercy perceived he was.

"Matthew, some people all over the world are dangerous like the green mamba because they lack patriotism. They killed their political and economic systems," Nelson observed, yawning. He seemed tired; but he will not say that out.

"We cannot run away from our continent, Africa, as Mercy suggests that we should run away from the garden because of the snake. We must stay to salvage Africa from the *wolves; the snakes,"* Matthew said.

"Yes, Africa must be made safe for all of us. We cannot continue to remain like this. *Awhiya-acha*! It's shameful!"

***

"Mine, so this man is dead?" Mercy asked Nelson in surprise.

"Yes, Ahmad Youssef, one of the leading lights of patriotism, has gone; gone forever."

"Do you remember you once spoke about him to me?"

"I do, and clearly. The day I kissed his picture in the paper I was reading. You were by my side."

"Yes." She was happy he remembered that without struggle.

"Youssef did a lot for Africa. He will live forever," Matthew remarked, stretching his hand for the radio from Nelson. He switched it on. News on the death of Ahmad Youssef was on air.

"Yes, his name will not be forgotten forever," Nelson agreed.

"This is a nugget of truth!" Matthew exclaimed.

"I have resolved to sensitize the students on the importance of patriotism. The on-going news is on Ahmad Youssef. Let us listen to it," Nelson advised. He never got tired with the news on the death of Ahmad Youssef. He would never.

"The government of the kingdom of Morocco has declared a 7-days mourning period for the death of Ahmad Youssef. The nation's flag will fly at half-

mast throughout this period of mourning. The government has also picked the 23rd day of September to commemorate late Ahmad Youssef yearly. Activities that will mark the celebration of this day will include lectures on the life and the core values of Ahmad Youssef with emphasis on patriotism and good governance. Only patriotic people, like Mo Ibrahim, Alhaji Aliko Dangote and Professor Patrick Loch Otieno Lumumba, who have practically demonstrated their love for Africa will deliver such lecture... "

"Africa is progressing," Nelson remarked as he listens to the news.

"How do you mean?" Matthew asked, reducing the volume of the radio and pressing down the antenna.

"Unpatriotic people will no longer be honoured to deliver lectures on lifestyles they haven't really lived themselves. Mo Ibrahim and few others, like Alhaji Aliko Dangote, an internationally acclaimed Nigerian industrialist, and Professor Patrick Loch Otieno Lumumba, the Kenyan, epitomes of good values and embodiments of patriotism, are the worthy Africans to deliver such lectures," Nelson explained.

"I know much about Alhaji Aliko Dangote because of his many productive investments in Nigeria and in other African countries, providing thousands of jobs for people and developing the economy of Africa. In this aspect, he is patriotic. He is a worthy son of Africa. I am also aware of Professor Patrick Loch Otieno Lumumba, the fierce campaigner for the entrenchment of patriotism in Africa. Tell me about the man, Mo Ibrahim," Matthew wanted to know.

"He is a Sudanese-British who has set up a foundation, Mo Ibrahim Foundation, to encourage good governance in Africa."

"He is a credible son of Africa, a patriot," Matthew remarked, squinting his eyes.

"He instituted Mo Ibrahim Prize for Achievement in African Leadership," Nelson revealed.

He prided himself as if Mo Ibrahim was his brother. He was. Both of them were Africans. Call them continental brothers if you may. But Nelson stood for universal brotherhood, too.

"What sort of achievements?"

"Good delivery on education, health and security; economic development and transfer of power by the rule of law."

"Only patriots will do these."

"That is why we are preaching patriotism," Nelson said, wishing other rich Africans would come up with similar initiatives like that of Mo Ibrahim to redeem the glorious image of Africa. He still resolved to sensitize the students on patriotism. He had not forgotten this, and he would not. It is like life to him.

FIVE

ஐஐ

The following day, after the day Ahmad Youssef passed on, Nelson, Mercy and Matthew were in the garden. Nelson's uncle later joined them.

The death of Ahmad Youssef still dominated their discussion. It was too early to abandon discussion on it. Nelson wouldn't just do that too soon. *Ko cekere,* even a little; he wouldn't. He revered the man so much to the extent of almost worshipping him. That would have been idolatry and he knew the danger of this. God says mankind should worship Him alone.

"Uncle is coming," Mercy said. Their eyes turned towards the direction where the old but agile and smart uncle was walking with imposing steps towards them. He walked briskly with a focused gaze, holding his head up. '*That is how a proud African son should walk,*' he would always say. He disliked sluggish and timid people.

"Good morning, my children," the uncle greeted.

"Good morning, uncle; you are welcome," they responded, arising to bow down as a mark of respect to greet him. It is an African tradition for the young people to greet the elders, bowing down as a sign of respect. This also has evolutionary elements of patriotism. A respectful son or daughter of Africa would not treat an elder with disrespect. Africans believe that a disrespectful son would not live long.

"Nooo, sit down," he said. But they won't. They'd rather stoop so low to complete the greeting. He blessed them, saying they shall be respected in their old age by the young ones as they did to him; he wished them long life and prayed that they would see their great grandchildren.

They told the uncle about the life and death of the great Moroccan. Uncle was silent all through the lectures without betraying his emotions. If an old man becomes emotional in the midst of the young, the young will be destabilized. It is unto him they depended for guidance in such distressful moments. He knew this. He gathered himself. Nelson had briefed him about Ahmad Youssef some time ago. That day, they were discussing on those that could pass as African patriots and Nelson had mentioned Ahmad Youssef. They discussed at length about him and Africa.

Kaba was the name of Nelson's uncle, his only surviving uncle. Like Walter Rodney, he discussed with Nelson, Mercy and Matthew about some African cultures that were being ignored like the robust ties that once existed among extended families. He also spoke of the past communal hunting, fishing and the beauty of work-teams that were all the social features of the African society before contact with the West; the contact which arrested the evolving civilization in Africa which was on the same pace with those of other worlds.

He spoke about the kinship that once existed in the life of Africans. He said these traits were the ones that brought harmony to the ancient African society. Nelson was vexed in spirit as he listened, not for vengeance but for inspiration to do something for the progress of Africa. He budged further and inclined his ears to listen well.

"Uncle, what really went wrong that these good and unifying things are not practiced anymore?" Nelson asked, his face wrinkling in sadness. He had been told of what happened but he wanted to know more.

"I have told you. It is the contact with the West. Some of the white men were brutal in spirit. They were brutal with some African traditional rulers who, in turn, were brutal with many of their subjects and sold them into slavery," he replied, asking Mercy to give him a cup of *agwadah* (a local drink made from guinea corn or maize or millet). It is mostly prepared by the *Koro*s. He had not taken anything that morning and his tummy rumbles in hunger. Mercy served him the *agwadah*.

"Thank you my daughter," uncle Kaba said after emptying the cup. They watched as he licked the pieces of the *agwadah* on the brim of the cup. He wanted more but was too timid to ask. Feeling refreshed again, he concentrated on the discussion.

"Take the cup, my daughter," uncle Kaba said, stretching the cup towards Mercy with his hand shaking. The cup fell off his hand and broke with a thud. Its pieces scattered all over the earth. The ceramic cup was a gift to Mercy on her wedding day. Uncle Kaba could feel the eyes staring through him. He moved to pick the pieces on the floor but the edges were sharp they could slice and pierce the skin. They must be picked carefully and immediately. Mercy stopped him. She would pick them.

"Uncle, it was my wedding gift. You will have to buy another one for me," Mercy gave out a long wail of despair. Uncle Kaba felt terribly sorry until Mercy suddenly exposed her teeth in a wide grin. She was surprised by how Uncle Kaba felt so remorseful.

"You were not so patriotic to handle it with care. That is how students and government workers do not handle government properties with patriotism," Mercy joked.

"Ha-ha-ha, my daughter; my son, your husband, will buy another one much better than this for you. I am sorry." He knew Mercy was joking with him as a daughter-in-law. They joked a lot.

"Uncle, uncle, I will buy a special cup which will be only for you. Even if you hit it on the floor, it will remain *kampe*, intact!"

"My daughter, it will be so kind of you. Don't hesitate to tell me whenever Nelson steps on your toe. I will be there for you anytime."

"Thank you, uncle," Mercy said while cautiously picking the broken pieces of the cup.

"Uncle, what misguided some of these white men?" Nelson would not leave him on this issue.

"Their ego; it misguided them. Today, some of them are regretting and are very remorseful. Some Africans are shamed too for they collaborated with the whites in carrying out this evil."

"Their ego," Nelson uttered, imagining the limitation of man.

As they were seated discussing, the birds perching on the trees in the garden began to twitter. The sounds were curiously unusual. A mist appeared suddenly and it impaired visibility. A windy atmosphere ensued, blowing the trees violently; yellow leaves fell off them and littered the garden, while some were blown away from the trees.

It was dry season but there was a cloud and lightning that traversed the sky.

Everyone expected the rain but it wasn't forthcoming. It wasn't the normal cloud usually seen during the rainy season. That was a mystery and it surprised everyone.

The wind hummed violently and caused the trees in the garden to swerve loosely, obeying the direction the wind blew their branches to. The whole place was blurry, taken over by thick mist. They ran for shelters in the hut and settled there. The hut was reserved for receiving visitors.

Uncle Kaba wondered and remarked that, "This is very unusual. *Uku (*an idol) must be consulted. It should know why all these things are happening."

"No, uncle, we don't believe in *uku*. We believe in the God of heaven and the earth, the living God," Mercy objected, shaking her head to affirm her objection.

"Stop that! If *uku* hears you, before tomorrow morning, you will be dead."

"*Sauwah Kinin!* Get away from here! *Uku* has no power over my life. I don't, and will never fear it."

Uncle Kaba pursed his lips and clenched his fist. His countenance turned grim and sad. How could a woman dishonor the ancestral god he grew up to see his people worshipping? However, Mercy would not cave in to him. She wished uncle Kaba was more enlightened to stop worshipping *uku*.

"Because you have been an obedient daughter-in-law, I will go to the shrine and appease *uku* to not harm you. But …"

"But what?" Mercy wanted to know, fixing her eyes on him.

"A goat, a he-goat, and five cocks must be brought by you for sacrifice. *Uku* will not receive less. On this, it has no mercy."

"I will not give anything. Let *uku* do its worst," Mercy insisted. Since the day she was born in the dispensary at *A-ha Fada,* thirty-seven years ago, her father, one of the early believers in the true God in Pa, immediately sounded these words as Godly seeds into her ears; *'Only the living God of the heavens and the earth is great and worthy of worship. He alone shall be the God you will worship and no other besides Him.'*

These words had remained in her mind since childhood. As she grew up, they solidly settled in her mind as engraved words on iron. Nothing would ever change her. Uncle Kaba realized this and he gave up, looking frustrated. He wished they had not discussed about *uku*.

Mercy urged uncle Kaba to forsake the African traditional religion.

"Uwa yian-nin (you this child) shut up your mouth! What do you know?" he objected. He wouldn't believe in the white man's Christianity. He said the white man used religion to cheat Africans through slavery and economic exploitation. He won't listen to the other side of the story which says there were two groups of white men that came to Africa; one, the slave traders who ravaged it with humiliation

in collaboration with mean or vain African kings; and the other, the missionaries who flooded it with light.

It was said that it was the mercantile activities of the slave traders that stained the good works of the missionaries. He wouldn't buy into this at all! Uncle Kaba said it was a distorted history. His stance on the issue intensified when he was told long ago that the missionaries consented to the inhuman system of slavery and brutality of slave traders; and who can tell whether the assertion is true? Nevertheless, the Whiteman's religion had brought light. The flesh, the flesh, that great enemy of man, might have intruded into it and stained it to the embarrassment of the missionaries who had good intentions.

"Uncle, some whites or institutions in the West have asked for forgiveness for their unfortunate involvement in slavery."

"And what are you saying?"

"Let us forget the past."

"Why?"

"Judgment and love are parallel. Only mercy and love meets; these last two bring harmony and harmony is for the progressives. You know that; don't you?" she waited for his response. None came. He would not just take that. There was still a long walk to cracking this nut— uncle Kaba's stance on the issue. Mercy suspended the matter.

***

Nelson smiled, mumbled some words and shook his head. His eyes pierced through the door and he noticed that the mist had disappeared. It retreated as if it had encountered some sort of defense against its offensive, the sort of British defense Hitler encountered in Britain under the motivational leadership of the great British statesman, Winston Churchill, during the Second World War. One could now see far and all round. It was exciting.

Nelson would not miss correlating this unusual misty weather to the lack of patriotism that hung as a mist over Africa, preventing it from really seeing what other continents had seen, and were seeing. He wished in silence, imagining;

"How impressive it will be if the unpatriotic darkness that hangs over Africa will similarly retreat as this mist has done to allow the light of patriotism to shine for the development of Africa."

The happiness of Nelson over the retreating mist was short lived. It was erased when he noticed that the fly of the national flag by the entrance of the door had been miraculously torn, almost centrally through the white stripe, into two parts.

The steel pole, on which it was hoisted, bent at about three-quarters of its length from the ground level. Another strange thing! He went back to his seat in the hut and sat down quietly, wondering over these unusual happenings— the chirping birds; the sudden mist that had receded, the windy weather that had ceased, the cloud, the lightning, the tearing of the fly of the national flag together with the bending of the steel pole.

All this while, Mercy and Matthew (uncle Kaba had left them) were silent, observing the restlessness of Nelson. They, too, were trying to figure out the meaning of all these unusual happenings. They are humans, and must wonder. Even animals do.

As usual, Nelson wouldn't stop questioning God.

"*Ate gashi*, God, what is the meaning of all these things?"

"God is pleased with him and wouldn't leave him in darkness." He answered him instantly through the blessed one, the angel.

"Nelson, the heavens must rejoice for the return home of Ahmad Youssef. The cloud, the lightning, the wind and the mist are the joyful manifestations of the heavens because a great man, Ahmad Youssef, has returned home to eternal rest. He made the world a better place. The heavens must celebrate his triumphal return in this manner."

"What can you say about the chirruping birds?" Nelson was not done yet.

"Why will the Nigerian birds not join the patriotic Moroccan birds to mourn the death of this great man? Right now, in the fortress of Timiderte, the interior of the Sarho Mountains and the high Atlas Range in Morocco, on their tops, the Moroccan birds have gathered in their multitude, weeping patriotically for the departure of Ahmad Youssef. He was known all over the continent. The birds, other animals, and even plants know this. As the heavens rejoice to have his spirit back, so is the soil to receive his remains. Everything returns to its source; spirit to spirit, dust to dust. But in what manner will the spirit return? Will it be in joy or in sorrow? Here is the importance of how one lives here on earth."

"One more question, the blessed one. Can I ask?"

"Go on. God does not want people to perish for lack of knowledge."

"Can you explain about the tearing of the fly of the flag and the bending of the pole?"

"They are for one and the same thing, the lack of national mourning for the passing on of Ahmad Youssef in solidarity with the Moroccan flag."

"ehnn!"

"Yes!"

"I can't understand this, the blessed one."

"Have you not seen the gathering of the heads of government?"

"Severally, my Lord,"

"They gather under their respective national flags, the symbols of their national identities as a people."

"What does that have to do with my question, Lord?"

"Good. It shows that the Nigerian people, as a nation, are not mourning with the Moroccan people because of the death of Ahmad Youssef."

"Thank you, Lord," Nelson said, satisfied.

"Ahmad Youssef was the best King Morocco never had," the angel said.

"I know; all Africans know this," Nelson agreed.

"Nelson, had you immediately made the flag to fly at half-mast when you heard about the death of Youssef, it wouldn't have been torn and the pole bent. To have it fly at half-mast is a sign of national mourning."

"I see."

"Yes. Do not forget this in future. Many aged patriotic Africans like Ahmad Youssef will soon be called to rest," the angel revealed. But don't be discouraged; the rising patriots; the rising patriots."

"Why, Lord? We need them to still guide us!"

"It is God that truly guide and guard. Don't worry. Once again, remember the rising African patriots. God will personally direct and guide them on what to do for this favoured but abused continent."

The discussion ended; Nelson was satisfied, wishing he could be in the beautiful mountainous Dominica, one of the West Indies islands in the Caribbean Sea, and all over the West Indies, to tell them about the rising African patriots. A great number of them were indigenous Africans— our brothers and sisters.The evil of slavery took them there. African culture had vanished among them with the passage of many generations. Many of them did not know of their true origins in Africa. It pained them as it pained us. They had imbibed the white man's culture and hardly thought of the African culture. They must be reclaimed and restored to African customs no matter their geographical locations. He wished to be there one day. A patriotic wish never fails; it always has the blessings of the heavens.

Nelson shook his head and adjusted the miniature flag on the table to its initial position. He did not know who had tampered with it. He knew proper arrangement of things gives clarity and efficiency. He would not compromise on this. He wished there would be one continental flag and one continental anthem for Africa to fulfill the dream of the founding pan-Africanists. He simply discarded the idea; no, he kept it aside with the hope for its achievement in future. For now, he would preach national and continental patriotism anyway, anywhere and to all classes of Africans. A crusader!

***

"What is it that is disturbing you, Mine?" Mercy asked. Nelson pretended not to hear her. His eyes were moving from Mercy to Matthew as if he was suspicious of them gossiping about him. His imagination took him to Kilimanjaro (now a dormant volcano), the highest mountain in Africa, also called the Roof of Africa, and to the Ethiopian Plateau at Ras Dashen where he imagined the birds of these countries had respectively gathered to mourn the death of Ahmad Youssef. He had been told that even the birds all over Africa were also mourning the great man; his imagination was, therefore in order.

He wished to live in the steps of Ahmad Youssef to be mourned at his death like that. He resolved to do so, vowing he would not be materialistic and would live a simple life like the great prophets that ever graced the earth. His imagination took him to Mount Everest (the Roof of the World) in the Himalaya range. He imagined birds flying over the mountain in serenity. He wished Asian and the other continents' birds would identify with African birds to mourn the death of Ahmad Youssef, wondering if there was racism among birds as in humans.

"I was about asking him that," Matthew joined, looking away from Nelson; he turned to look at a bird that just perched on a guava tree in the garden, trying to eat some of its fruits.

Nelson kept quiet.

"Are you hearing us?" Mercy asked, and drew a dustpan to put the pieces of the ceramic cup, the one uncle Kaba had broken. They had been kept beside her since she picked them.

"I was wondering what had just happened," he finally said, scratching his chin. It was itching him. He sustained a wound on it yesterday when he was shaving. It was a pimpled chin, the discomfort of hairy men.

"The songs of the birds, the mist, the wind, the…?" Matthew asked.

"And the meanings of the cloud and the lightning?" Mercy added, looking intently at Nelson.

"What can you say about that?" Matthew asked sarcastically.

"I questioned God and the angel of the LORD told me the meaning of all these."

"What did the angel tell you?" Mercy asked, visibly surprised and anxious to hear from him.

He narrated to them all what he had been told. They went out and found that the fly of the flag was torn into two and the steel pole bent as he said. They were afraid.

"I did question God on these things but He wouldn't answer me. I am sure Matthew, you also did," Mercy complained.

"I did. God didn't answer me either," Matthew confirmed.

"Nelson, why will God answer you alone?" Mercy asked; she sounded envious but fearful of the rebuke of God; she is very familiar with the consequences of the attack of Aaron and Miriam on Moses, the man God had chosen to use; the most humble of men on earth; it was God that said so, and His judgment is perfect. Don't question Him or He will ask you some questions that you cannot answer; accept it as it is with faith! God had said it and so it is; just believe, a simple thing but men find it difficult to do so.

"It is because of my sincere love for Africa."

"Julius," Matthew called, "you are a blessed person for God to respond to you. But Mercy and I also love Africa." Their love for Africa was not yet as deep as Nelson's for God to answer them. They knew this.

"Can't you take just a simple instruction, Matthew? Don't ever call me that name again. Understand?" Nelson warned.

"Sorry, please."

"How can one progress by looking back? I am now Nelson. I can't be Julius anymore. It will be retrogressive. Don't you see that?"

"I am really sorry, please," Matthew pleaded, feeling foolish; he had been warned before.

"Africans must not look back to the days of stagnation. Forward, forward, we must move if there will be any progress," Nelson said, his nerves calm. He divested himself of his Chinese suit and hung it on a dry branch close by. The weather was hot.

"Mine, God lifted you above us," Mercy said, her face somber from worrying if Nelson will turn out boastful. But Nelson was a humble man. He would not take pride in looking down on any man.

"An Indian proverb says," Nelson started, *'There is nothing noble in being superior to others. True nobility lies in being superior to your former self.'* He smiled furtively as he imagined the debasing nature of social stratification in the world.

"What do you mean by 'your former self'?" Matthew demanded. He couldn't relate to it.

"You don't understand this? It means rising beyond one's weaknesses," Nelson answered.

"Such as?" Matthew pushed further.

Mercy was silent but attentive even while tying her scarf; the wind had blown it off from her head into the garden. She was aware the moment it got blown off, but she couldn't go for it. When life is threatened, any other thing is valueless. So, patriotism must be earnestly pursued.

"Slavery was a bad institution the white man created. It is bad that some African traditional rulers aided the white men to enslave their African brothers, sisters, sons and daughters. It is also bad that some white men continue to treat the black man as inferior and less human than they are. It is a weakness if Africans continue to live with malice over slavery and colonialism. It is weakness for any race to accept that it is inferior to other races. Exploitation of other races for economic gains hampers universal unity and development. It is a weakness on the human race if it lacks empathy. We must rise above those debased attitudes," Nelson explained knowing he had not satisfied Matthew's curiosity. He was right.

"Mention other weaknesses, please," Matthew pleaded.

"Envy, economic and political and social racism, terrorism, hatred, idleness, vengeance, insincerity, bad leadership etc.," he added.

"Nothing makes a man fundamentally different from another, no matter his race, absolutely nothing!" Matthew said.

"No more of this, Matthew; no more. However, Africans must leave the valley and climb the mountain of development. The Europeans, the Americans and the Asians are moving ahead in their developmental strides. We must be there," Nelson said, wishing for the integration of African economies for effectiveness and for the rejection of external economic policies that are exploitative.

Nelson hated being entangled by the misfortunes of the past no matter how painful they were. However, it annoyed him whenever he thought of how the black man aided the white man to enslave his own brother and sister. He had been told that there was a time when the progressive white man saw slavery as barbaric and called for its abolition, some black men opposed the move for they were profiting from its debased economic gains. Therefore, for him, both the white man and the black collaborator were guilty.

Even though Nelson regrettably believed that the African traditional ruler should be judged and mildly punished for not loathing the inhuman slavery activities of the white man, he believed that the white man is to be judged greatly, sentenced and fined for this dark period that dwarfed African development.

Why this verdict? Look at it this way:

'The enslaving white man, the African traditional ruler as the white man collaborator and the African subject were like three moving vehicles, following each other directly on the same lane with the African subject in the front, followed by the African traditional ruler and lastly, the white slave master. The slave master, because of his ego, refused to drive well (live in civility) and hit the vehicle of the African traditional ruler. The traditional ruler's vehicle surged, staggered and hit the vehicle of the African subject off the road and into the bush, a strange land, the white man's country. Who then is the cause for this unfortunate accident?'

'The whiteman! Therefore, he is causally guilty of the offence. He is to be blamed.' But Nelson was sympathetic enough to forgive the white man and only wanted reconciliation with the white man who was brutal and cruel because of his ego.

Nelson's belief in the reconciliation of the black man and the whiteman for offences of slavery was propped by late Nelson Mandela's statement on the marble which says, '*Resentment is like drinking poison and then hoping it will kill your enemies,* '[1] and by the eternal truth of the supremacy of forgiveness over vengeance.

Nelson believed that no amount of reparation will compensate for the lost African souls in the Atlantic, the dehumanization of slaves in European plantations and the lost lineal identity of the descendants of enslaved Africans. He felt that the dignity of man is priceless. It is sacred. When it is tampered with, the remedy is sincere repentance for forgiveness. The offended party should forgive even if the offending party refuses to repent.

That was Nelson's stance on this protracted issue; that the black man should forgive the white man; that the white man should desist from all forms of neo-colonialism. The relationship should be symbiotic and not parasitic which was reminiscent of the epochs of slavery and colonialism.

Nelson believed that for the sake of the few dissenting voices for slavery like Lord Mansfield, the Messiah of the slaves, and Abraham Lincoln and other Europeans and Africans who spoke out against slavery, Africans should not sink deep into hate by still holding on to this most unfortunate period in the history of humanity. He believed it was worthwhile if Africans could help erase the guilt the white man still felt over slavery by forgiving him. Love conquers all. That is the principle of *Satyagraha* practiced by M. K. Gandhi to win independence for Indians from the British with no violence. This will be progress for Africa and the whole world.

"The campaign for patriotism in Africa by Africans must continue," Nelson maintained. His eyes were heavy and his head light, he took his leave with no excuse, for a snooze.

SIX

ᙘᙓ

The earth had received its own portion of Ahmad Youssef. His death left African patriots shaken to the spine. His remains vibrated with joy in his grave for the victorious home coming. Death lingered in the air, making Africa dull and lifeless. Nelson meditated on how the priest will always utter "dust to dust" just before internment. Then mourners would temporarily get into their senses for as long as the funeral lasted. Some shedding tears and weeping, others shaking their heads in disbelief, wondering how life quickly disappeared; some sighing with contempt at this surreal life, uttering in discontent;

"*Life is vanity, vanity and absolutely vanity.*"

Then, shortly afterwards, we forget too quick that we were once mourning and live our lives unheeding death as if nothing ever happened. We will again debase our thoughts, speeches and actions from the moral heights we have raised them when those solemn words "dust to dust" were pronounced by the priest. That was the way of the unpatriotic persons, the way of those who do not truly fear their creator, the God of the universe.

***

On a Wednesday, the thirty-third day of the passing on of Ahmad Youssef, Nelson was going to teach history to the students. He had spent the evening of the previous day, preparing the lesson notes, lacing them with ideas on patriotism. It was easy for him to do so because of materials in his library. He kept his books on a shelf, a wooden one, with two columns and three rows in each column that was placed to the wall in Nelson's living room. Shelved in one column were books on different subjects arranged in their categories to ease searching. The other column was stacked with files, containing valuable documents; some contained seminar papers; some, speeches he had delivered on several occasions on patriotism; some, history and geography separately.

Nelson was ready to leave for school. He wished his wife a good day, patted her on the back and disappeared into the open.

Mercy smiled her eyes bright and her cheeks were glowing in pride. She watched him walk out of the gate and blessed the day she met him. She returned to her stool and continued soaking *gero* (cereal that is like millet) in a small rubber bucket, urging their little children who were sitting in the kitchen to take their breakfast quickly so as not to be late for school.

"Ushiwinin; Uyinshi, eat quickly so that you will not be late," she told them.

Uyinshi, the younger one, a female, crammed the food. Ushiwinin, the brother, shouted at her, raising his hand to beat her but halted abruptly— his hand and anger too. He was a gentle and sympathetic boy. Uyinshi shouted in fear. Their mother heard and rebuked them. Ushiwinin told her why they were quarrelling.

"You must stop that bad character henceforth. You must stop being greedy," Mercy warned, pointing at Uyinshi. She was angered by this. "I am telling you the truth. We have to teach you moderation and love in all you do right from this age. If you love your brother, you will not like to cram the food denying him what to eat."

She cried, refusing to eat.

Mercy didn't give Uyinshi even a tinge of attention. She knew that she would come looking for food when she got hungry. Mercy was however pained in her heart for she loved her children dearly even though they must be disciplined.

"If you can love each other, you will also extend your love to the world. You will not be selfish but patriotic," she told the kids, gave them some chocolates and walked them out of the house. She stood watching as they wobbled out of the gate.

"Thank you mummy," they chorused. Uyinshi had now forgotten the stern rebuke of her mother. Children can easily forgive after being angered and move on. We, Africans, must forgive ourselves and the whites alike, and like children, we must shed our misery and move on. The heavens love children's forgiving spirit. That is why the kingdom is said to belong to them. It is a kingdom of LOVE where patriotism thrives everywhere.

"Don't worry, my dear. Behave well in the school so that you will not spoil our family's name. If you behave well, you will grow up unable to sully Nigeria's and Africa's name, and that is patriotism."

"What is Africa, mummy?" Uyinshi asked. She had heard about Nigeria; Africa, no; she had not; it was too much for her age.

"You must continue to leave now. You are getting late. When you return I will explain to you. Okay?"

"Yes, mummy," they responded and continued to leave for the school with their school bags on their backs.

***

Mercy intended to use as a visual aid, the map of Africa that had each country coloured, to make Uyinshi understand the meaning of Africa. She would tell her that all the countries in the map together made up Africa. She was a teacher. She would do it better. The children had discovered their father was sad and they had asked her why. She would use this opportunity to point out to them the geographical location of Morocco and to tell them that their father was sad because of the death of a good man there who loved Africa. With that, she would tell them to be good Africans as they grow up.

Imparting knowledge on patriotism to the young was necessary.

***

The history lesson had gone very far. Nelson was taking the class through pockets of pre-slavery, slavery and post slavery; pre-colonial, colonial and post-colonial epochs in African history, lacing it with the stories of acts of patriotism by patriots. He was fair to tell the class that some whites loved Africans and would like to see Africa progress. He told them that only obstinate whites were racial.

"Do you understand why patriotism is non-negotiable no matter the circumstances one is faced with?" Nelson asked the students, wondering whether they understood.

"Yes, we do," they chorused. He told them that lack of patriotism was the bane to Africa's development, and not that Africans were in anyway less intelligent. He gave examples of African inventors; some in Africa and some in Diaspora.

"You must be the disciples of Ahmad Youssef by now; I am one already. You must be patriotic to make Africa great."

"Yes, sir! We will be patriotic," they chorused loudly, drawing the attention of Ego Yero, the principal, who was passing by in his routine surveillance of teachers to check whether they were in their classes, teaching the students or not. He had noticed Nelson's dedication to his work. Due to this, he hardly bothered to check up on him.

But on this fateful day, he entered the class and saw the word 'PATRIOTISM' boldly written on the blackboard.

"That is good, Nelson. Teach them to grow up to be patriotic Africans. They may be the ones to redeem Africa." Turning to the students, he said, "Love Africa; love Africa. You cannot be patriotic without love for Africa. To love Africa is to do the right thing and to protect it from being destroyed economically and from being messed up politically and socially."

"We will love Africa! We will love Africa, sir!" they chorused.

"That is good," he said and moved out of the class with a self-satisfied feeling that the school was raising patriotic children.

The principal left the class with confidence that Nelson will instill patriotic spirit into the students because he had demonstrated that before.

A story was told of how Nelson, some years ago, vehemently opposed illegal mining of tourmaline (a type of gemstone) in the slopes of Pa hills by a foreign mining company. Unpatriotic locals had collaborated with the foreign company to do the illegal mining. He wanted the mining of the mineral to be done in compliance with the mining laws, and for the benefit of the country and all other stakeholders. When the company and the locals that collaborated with it refused to listened to him, he reported the case to the responsible regulatory agency of the government. The company and the locals that were involved were penalized in accordance with the provisions of the mining laws.

"I like the way you responded to the principal. I am really happy," Nelson commended the class, going round to shake their little hands in utter delight. He shook thirty-three hands without stopping.

"Thank you, sir."

"Class," Nelson called, "I have a piece here by the great writer, Ngugi wa Thiong'o, a Kenyan. It seems to be calling for patriotism in Africa.

"For Africa, the key thing is to secure our natural resources, our economic environment, our polity, our culture. If you can secure that base, each country and also we, the continent of Africa, can engage with other continents, on the basis of give and

take. But just now, the problem is that within Africa, we don't even make use of our own resources-we negotiate a price for them!

"But we don't manufacture with our resources. I would like to see Zambia making things with the copper, South Africa having companies, making use of their gold, and Nigeria with oil refineries making products with their oil. I want to see manufacturing all over Africa using our resources, instead of simply negotiating their price. I would like to see factories owned by African entrepreneurs making things with that material, with the resources of simply negotiating a price. We have to become a continent of makers, not just a continent that sets its price for its raw materials. Africa has always given to the west; Africa must learn to give to itself; the working millions. That will be what will make Africa a big global player.

"Another thing would be to get our politicians to debate about policy, not about which ethnic group your opponent comes from. You want to know from the politicians what their policy is for the poor in the country. We must eradicate poverty, ignorance and disease. A people-based African union would help to realize this on a continental level."[1]

The class was silent; you could hear a pin drop. Then a student's hand quivered in the air.

"No questions yet, please," Nelson said, flipping through a file. He brought out a paper. "You will do well to listen to this too," he said and began to read from the paper.

"We cannot continue to export bauxite and then in return import alumina to feed our local aluminum smelter. We need to work towards creating an integrated bauxite and aluminum industry in

Ghana.... As a president and a father, I owe my children- my sons and my daughter -and all the children of Ghana to create for them a country where they can walk with their dignity intact and their heads held high and stand shoulder to shoulder with the children of Europe, South America, Asia, North America and the rest of the world," John Dramani Mahama, President of Ghana, worried on Ghana's lack of benefiting much from its natural resources while addressing UN General Assembly in September, 2013.

"Any question?" Nelson asked. The boy that raised his hand earlier on raised it again.

"Yes, ask your question."

"You said that some whites love Africans and will like to see us progressing. How? You cannot easily sell this to us, sir," the boy said with an obvious frown, the type that will send a child quivering.

"Why?"

"They enslaved our people; lynched mutinous slaves over fire; they destroyed African civilizations; they practiced racial, economic and social injustices on Africans and many other evils; no, sir! No, it is difficult believing this. How do they love Africans if they did all these to us?" Martin, the boy, insisted.

"Martin," Nelson called, "it is not all the whites. We have those who think differently among them even in those dark days. Today, today, there is considerable improvement on the recognition of the dignity of man from any race."

"Give us examples of such people?"

"There are many. I will give you some examples."

Nelson opened his folder that had historical extracts from different sources and gave the class the following examples to show that some of the whites positively identified with Africans, suffered together with Africans in the fight for civil rights, and some of them even died in the process.

"Lord Mansfield," Nelson began, "who judged against slavery in the case between an African slave, James Somerset and his master, Charles Steward. There won't be details here. The judgment set slave trade on the path of eradication. Having followed how the lawyers to James Somerset argued, Lord Mansfield ruled as follows:

'The state of slavery is such a nature that it is incapable of being introduced on any reason , moral or political; but only positive law, which preserves its force long after the reasons, occasion, and time itself from whence it was created, is erased from memory. It's so odious, that nothing can be suffered to support it, but positive law. Whatever inconveniences, therefore, that may follow from this decision, I cannot say this case is allowed or approved by the law of England; and therefore, the Black must be discharged.'[2]

This ruling was in 1772. Nelson proceeded with the second example.

"The American Civil War was because of slavery. The Southern States did not like the abolition of slavery as did the Northern States. Because of that, the south seceded, causing the civil war. Abraham Lincoln was US President then. He opposed slavery, too. Thirdly, listen to this,"

'One of the most significant facts of the historic March on Washington was that one quarter of the people gathered together were whites - marking their first large scale participation in the civil rights movement. They had been moved by the events of

Birmingham – and so had the rest of the nation. That summer, President Kennedy proposed to Congress the most comprehensive, far-reaching civil rights legislation ever conceived. By the fall, schools across the South were integrated without even the slightest hint of violence.'[3]

"Here is the fourth:

".... After these meetings, Lyndon Johnson addressed the U.S. Congress and proposed a comprehensive voting rights bill aimed at protecting African- Americans 'right to vote." 'All of us must overcome the crippling legacy of bigotry and injustice,' he said. 'And we shall overcome.' "Johnson's use of the slogan of the civil rights movement gave African-Americans a big boost in morale while, at the same time, disheartening the white opposition in Alabama.... In the days and months that followed, Martin King's stirring oratory gave way to the realization that the Selma campaign had, indeed, significantly moved the needle of progress in the right direction. For the first time, huge numbers of white were supporting the mission of the movement. That, in and of itself, was a monumental achievement. But even more significant was the fact that the United States Congress, that summer, passed the Voting Rights Act of 1965 which Lyndon Johnson signed into law on August 6.

"'*But, once again, there was a price that had to be paid by those who had pressed for change and progress. Two white ministers were clubbed in the streets of Selma and one of them, Reverend James Reed, died as a result of his injuries. A white housewife named Viola Liuzzo was killed by members of the Klan as she transported marchers back to Selma....*'"[4]

"Fifthly, in the recent past, in the 1990s," Nelson continued, "Sedick Isaac, a progressive South African white, an activist, campaigned for the abolition of the South African apartheid regime. He was sentenced for sabotage and imprisoned in Robben Island in 1964 to a 12-year prison term which was increased in 1969 for operating a private radio while in the prison to be current with world affairs," Nelson concluded and closed the folder.

"Class, do you understand?"

They chorused in affirmation.

"So, some of these whites are good," the boy that asked the question said.

"Oh, yes!" Nelson exclaimed.

"Sir, Ngugi wa Thiong'o seems to present a blue print for the development of Africa, the addition of value to our raw materials before selling the products; can we get there?" a girl asked. It was a mixed school.

"I spoke about the rising African patriots. When they come to lead we will get there," Nelson answered, turned suddenly towards the window and said, "they are coming," smiling in hope meditatively.

"Who are coming, sir?" the students asked.

He gestured for the class to come over the window and see the patriots coming. They rushed to the window. Turn by turn, in convenient groups of not more than four, they looked through the window on the directive of Nelson, but only two girls, Salome and Dana, could see them. The rest could not see. Although, they were children, Salome and Dana were patriotic.

Salome and Dana would not throw pieces of paper anyhow in the school compound. They would not waste the water in the cistern. They were careful with the books given them. Whenever the national anthem was sung, they would always stand motionless. They would always pick littered pieces of papers and other rubbish seen in the school compound. Salome was heard one day rebuking a boy for breaking a table, saying that government properties must be taken care of. Both Salome and Dana had demonstrated spirit of patriotism. They love their school, Nigeria and Africa. The heavens were pleased with them and opened their eyes to see the rising African patriots. Like begets like, they say. The other students could not see and they demanded to know why.

"Only people who love Africa are allowed to have this vision. You must be patriotic students to be attended to by the heavens," Nelson told them and asked them to go back to their seats.

"Class, listen to me attentively. Though some white men and some black men caused us to be this underdeveloped, present trends are indicating that we are moving out of this unfortunate situation after a long walk. These words of the global man, our icon, the late Nelson Mandela, must be embedded in our hearts." He kept quiet for a while as if he was in a trance.

"Tell us, sir! Tell us! We love him. He had done Africa proud," the students were all excited.

"Yes, he did. Even whites scrambled to shake hands with Madiba. It was a blessing to them, to everybody, to shake hands with him. How did it feel shaking me few minutes ago? You believe I am an important man, don't you?"

"Yes, you are! We felt good!"

"Yes, that was how the whites and the blacks, everybody, felt when they had opportunity to shake hands with the great man, the patriotic African, Madiba. I did not have the opportunity to shake hands with him but I kissed his picture in a newspaper. He was a sage."

"Sir, tell us what Mandela said!" the students demanded enthusiastically.

"I will tell you but you must be ready to walk by it though I know it is not easy."

"We will! We will!" the students chorused out of excitement.

"That is good. Hear what he said as he walked out of prison."

Nelson began to read from a paper he pulled out of a file.

'As I walked out the door toward the gate that would lead to my freedom, I knew if I didn't leave my bitterness and hatred behind, I'd still be in prison.'[5]

"Class, what a great man he was!" Nelson exclaimed, returning the paper into the folder.

Africans must walk out of the *prison* of underdevelopment to freedom without bitterness and hatred for any race. Like Mandela, we must forgive and build a rainbow world for all the people of the earth to live in harmony and dignity. We are strong to do this because it is not something for the weak. That is the best homage we can give to this man.

"Like Ngugi wa Thiong'o and the Ghanaian president bemoaned the lack of adding value to our raw materials before selling them, I place this as a challenge to all of you. As from today, think of how you are going to achieve this. Among you, are the rising African patriots. You must be good leaders to achieve this."

"Yes, sir, we will."

"Nelson Mandela will not stop being our reference point. He will continue to be. Mandela said, *'a leader is like a shepherd. He stays behind the flock, letting the most nimble go out ahead, where upon the others follow, not realizing that all along they are being directed from behind.'* He also said, *'overcoming poverty is not a task of charity, it is an act of justice. Like slavery and apartheid, poverty is not natural. It is man-made and it can be overcome and eradicated by the actions of human beings. Sometimes it falls on a generation. You can be that generation. Let your greatness blossom'*[6]

"Class, your generation can be that generation Mandela said," Nelson said, his eyes sweeping over the class as if expecting questions from students. None came.

"We have had enough on patriotism today. You must be patriotic enough to be able to have your *'heads held high and stand shoulder to shoulder with the children of Europe, South America, Asia, North America and the rest of the world,'"* Nelson repeated the words of John Dramani Mahama, the President of Ghana.

"Pray for us, teacher," the students said with palpable solemnity.

"I will, I will. I must if I will be credible to say like Dr. William Edward Burghardt Du Bois, the founder of modern pan-Africanism, that *'Now my life will flow on in the vigorous young stream of Ghanaian life which lifts the African personality to its proper place among men. And I shall not have lived and worked in vain.'*[7]

Nelson told the class that he was pouring his life into them. And he prays that this will flow into the lives of all Africans as well, making them patriotic so as to place Africa on a dignified plain among men.

"We will be patriotic to work for Africa's dignity. No going back! We will never!" the students promised.

SEVEN

ꕥ

In an open field, a fallowed land lay neglected for years with nothing but trees scattered over it; mostly locust bean trees with canopies extending over the earth, where people always ran to for relaxation and shelter from the scorching sun. Mahogany trees surrounded the environment. They were used for timber, making lumbering a lucrative business for some enterprising people in Pa village and environs. Before felling any tree, obligations on rules of forestry had to be fulfilled. Pockets of anthills distracted the flat topography of the land. Termites descending from their anthills ravaged crops anytime the field was cultivated. This was one of the reasons why it had been abandoned for some years. Nelson went there early in the morning in order to meditate quietly on Africa and how Africa would be made great through monumental acts of patriotism.

He heard noise and shrill voices echoing in the bush close by. He observed and noticed some persons felling mahogany trees while talking in loud indistinct tones. As they lumber huge trees, loud thuds of falling trees echoed throughout the forest. Two persons from the group were tending a fire, cooking, a little distance away from the group. The youngest was fetching firewood in tattered and soil-stained clothes. He dropped the logs of woods and trailed a mouse he saw wandering wearily. He fell into a gully and lost his target. His legs were all bruised with the right leg fractured. Nelson helped them apply a twine to the fractured leg to arrest the blood gushing out generously. They ceased work that day because of the accident and immediately rushed the patient to a traditional doctor for attention.

Nelson placed a mat made from green leaves broken from shrubs under the shade of one of the trees. As he lay on the mat, his mind fluttered in joy while his soul felt an indescribable peace that was totally elevating. Through continental networking, much had been done since then to sensitize people on the need for mental decolonization and patriotism. He would not compromise his stance on the issue of reconciliation between Africa and the West. Evil had been done and Africans were wounded but he believed Africans should rise above malice because it was retarding to keep dwelling on that, seeking sympathy. However, he would not also compromise his stance against all forms of racism. He wanted the West to be freed from this, too. The West needed to see that all men— black, white, and red are equal. He hoped that an army of progressive whites would arise to perform this noble task to set the West free from the shackles of racism. The West thinks she is free whereas she is not. He said racism enslaved its practitioners; that the West should know that freedom was not to be entangled by any form of evil. He believed that racism in all forms was evil. Nelson understood it that way and he believed it could not be mired by anybody upon the face of the earth.

Nelson was truthful; he would not deny that some Africans were contributing to the ills of Africa. For this, he would not tolerate the unprogressive Africans who were not patriotic and who continued to plunder the economies of Africa, at the same time aide the West exploit Africa. He meditated on these matters until he fell asleep under the cool shade of the tree. The surrounding was recreational, especially with the air blowing coolly and gently and the trees bending to the waves. It was a nice place to commune with nature and learn lots of lessons from the silence in the forest, the chirping of birds, the humming of wind and the sparkling greens of trees.

The sun was setting slowly. Across the plains of Pa village to the west, Nelson watched as the yellow sun set slowly, preparing to vanish to another part of the world. He knew it was now time to go back home. As he trailed the bush path, returning home, he imagined how robust Africa's economy would be if there should be free movement of people, capital, services and goods among African markets. He imagined how African traditions and social standards could be restored for development by reversing the partitioning of Africa which was done at the Berlin conference of 1884-1885 orchestrated by Portugal and facilitated by the German Chancellor, Otto Von Bismarck.

The Berlin Conference was the conference in which the continent of Africa was balkanized into 50 states like the wrinkling of a plain of loamy soil under the attack of the cold and windy harmattan, blowing across the Sahara, unsettling clouds of dust, blowing rooftops off houses and, violently uprooting trees, as it blew towards the coastal areas. But it did not get there. It mostly stopped at the Savannah regions.

Yes, it was geopolitical harmattan that blew across Africa from the Berlin Conference, the *political Sahara*, which dismembered Africa into political enemies and blew off Africa, the roof that was once a canopy for all, and for imperialist interests. But still, Nelson would not be so debased to harbor malice against anyone. Forgiveness was his drink. However, he wished that racial equality be achieved.

Nelson had with him a copy of the New African Magazine. He stopped on the way to read what Tito Alai wrote in it.

"The common thread that ties Africa's fragmented historical narrative together is the subtext of African inferiority, across the board, which pervades Africa's historiography. The accepted picture that emerged was based on anecdotal accounts of events, which sought to portray European adventurers, explorers, missionaries and settlers as the heroes of the piece. This narrative, once established, became the foundation of the character campaign that continues to this day.

"You will no doubt have heard the maxim 'perception is reality'. Global perception has been conditioned to accept that everything about Africans is inferior: African traditions are inferior, African music is inferior, African languages are inferior, African education is inferior, African spiritual belief is inferior, African management is inferior... there is no end to the list, all these items adding up to sum total conclusion that Africans are indeed inferior."[1]

Nelson was disturbed on this. But he was quickly comforted when he recalled that a progressive and unbiased Mr. Clinton, an American, once told him that it was Dr. Hale Williams, the son of a freed slave, that performed the first successful open heart surgery operation in the USA; that it was Dr. Garret Morgan, the son of a slave, that invented the gas mask and the first traffic light, and that it was an African-American, Benjamin Banneker, who helped in the designing of the US Congress Capitol building in Washington DC. With these recollections, Nelson faulted the wrong perception on Africans. However, Nelson believed patriotism was still lacking in Africa. He wanted to see Africans placing premium value on making a name in the development of Africa than enriching their personal bank accounts to the detriment of the national economies. He said Africans must sell themselves with the commodity of patriotism by re-orienting their minds, as Carter G. Woodson, the father of Black History Month (BHM), now known as African-American History Month, advocated many years ago.

As he went home, he came to a stream close to the village. It is called *Idafu.* Its source was a hill in the northern part of Jeri town. Pa was situated in the south of Jeri town. The stream was adorned by green trees on its banks all through the year. The water was therefore always cool and the villagers also drank from there. Nelson decided to bathe there.

He cupped a handful of water and splashed it over his frame, uttering these words, *'God, splash patriotism on Africa to wash away from her all ills, internally or externally caused, as the dirt from my body is being washed now, so that Africa will progress.'*

After another splash of water he continued;

'God wash down the ills of all forms of racism and imperialism from the West so that they will truly have real freedom, freedom of conscience.' After another splash of water, he said, *'God wash Africa and all the other continents of hatred so that we will relate with one another in the real sense of brotherhood without political and economic sabotage of one another.'*

He alternated these words after each splash of water on his body. God listened to his supplication and sent an angel to minister to him.

***

At night, after Nelson returned from meditating in the bush, he sat in his garden all alone still meditating on the ills of Africa when an angel appeared to him in a vision in the form of an African map having clumps of people at some rivers and lakes in Africa. He was in the spirit. *'What is the meaning of this, Lord?'* he asked.

The vision was taken away.

With a strong inclination that the angel would appear again to him in a vision, Nelson, on the following day and at the same time, went and sat in the garden. The moon was out and shining. He thought of the possible meaning of the vision from yesterday night. Instead of giving him the answer, the angel appeared to him in another vision. This time, it was a vision of the map of Africa with undimmed lights and people from different corners of the world trooping to it.

'What is this again, Lord?' he asked.

A voice whispered to him, *'hold your peace.'*

On the third night, Nelson was in the garden at the same time as the day before. The moonlight shone grey flickers on the trees and flowers. He sat down to meditate and suddenly an immense cloud with flashing lightning appears. The cloud appeared in a bolt, with the image of a man in it emitting sparkles of light. An angel had taken the form of man to reveal himself to Nelson. He told Nelson the meaning of the vision he was given.

"Nelson, the man that loves Africa from the heart," the angel called.

"Yes, speak for I am listening, my Lord."

"I am here, in the cold night to tell you the meaning of the first vision. I am revealing these things to you because you are a credible associate of heaven to make Africa and the whole world a better place; you are, indeed, a true disciple of Ahmad Youssef. The heaven is well pleased with you."

"Thank you so much, my Lord. I am humbled."

"Yes, you deserve it for you are worthy."

"Thank you, the blessed one."

"Now in the first vision, the groups of people gathered at different points around African rivers and lakes are the gathering of African nationals, mostly the poor, sitting by the different rivers and lakes of their respective nations, weeping."

"I am listening, the blessed one." Both surprise and sadness were his countenance.

"They are weeping because they have been told of how early civilizations of Africa were destroyed; how Africans were ferried across the Atlantic Ocean to the so called "new world" to be exploited productively on the plantations; how Africa was partitioned to serve the economic and political interest of the West; how Africans are still colonized mentally; how the Bretton Woods institutions' Structural Adjustment Programmes were imposed on African states with dire consequences on African economies; how most African leaders are still serving the interests of the West over the sovereign rights of their people; how most of the earth's resources are housed in Africa, yet Africa has the lowest bank account; how the West deems Africans as an inferior race and how Africans fan this prejudice by being underdeveloped."

"Lord, I know they will also weep about African leaders allowing international corporations to maintain off-shore accounts while corrupting African economy."

"Nelson, it is one of the things that hurt them. They remembered many bad things, things that retarded the development of Africa and are weeping, washing their faces at intervals to continue to weep. There is no one to comfort them. But God will soon comfort them. He will soon visit Africa with glory."

"Thank you, Lord. Thank you, Lord," Nelson said, bowing in worship of God.

"Now, come with me. I am taking you to these places where the people are weeping." Nelson joined the cloud and off they went.

***

"This is the Volta River in Ghana. This place is just some distance from the confluence of the Black Volta and White Volta. What can you see?"

"I can see men, women and children all in Ghanaian *Kente*, weeping; poor people."

"Yes, you are correct. They are also weeping for the Ghanaian economy that is presently not well standing on its feet."

On the Volta River, Nelson saw fishermen, paddling wooden canoes and checking their fishing nets. The river was flowing still as if mourning with the crying Ghanaians. Yes, even nature despises injustice.

The angel took him to another place.

***

"Where are we now, Lord?"

"We are at Orange River in the Northern Cape province of South Africa. We are close to P.K Rouxdam."

"We are in South Africa?" he asked.

"Yes, the former apartheid state."

"Take me to Qunnu, the village of Nelson Mandela in the Eastern Cape province of South Africa; the blessed village that once gathered prominent people during Mr. Mandela's burial."

"For your patriotic spirit, I will do that. But for now what do you see here?"

"A multitude of people weeping," Nelson answered, tears dropping down his face. They mourned while chanting sorrowful songs reminiscent of those sang during apartheid regime. In their songs they said they were yet to see the dividends of freedom from apartheid. They said their freedom was not yet complete because economic apartheid was still a yoke on them. They said there was poverty all over the land. The angel took him to Qunnu.

***

"This is Qunnu, the home of Mandela," the angel announced.

"I am gladdened, Lord. I am satisfied, Lord. Let me now die, Lord."

"Your time has not come, Nelson. You still have an assignment to accomplish here on earth."

"Let the will of God be fulfilled in my life."

"Let me take you to where he was laid to rest," the angel said.

***

"This is Nelson Mandela's resting place."

"You, the blessed one, remain in peace. I am here with an angel of the LORD. God is going to bring the Africa of your dream to existence. Many patriots are coming to rule Africa," Nelson said, almost kneeling to worship and he quickly remembered that God alone is to be worshipped. He discarded the idea immediately.

"Let us go, Nelson. I know you are now happy to see the home of your namesake."

"Yes, Lord; yes, Lord," He said, his heart longing to remain in Qunnu for the rest of his life to feel the aura of Mandela's glory. But he must move and they moved on.

***

"This is Lake Kivu in Rwanda. It is good to note that it lies between this country and the Democratic Republic of Congo."

Lake Kivu had a serene environment that was a great spot for relating with nature and was fertile for agriculture, too. Many Rwandans gathered and wept because of the unfortunate genocide of the 1990s when the Tutsi and the Hutsi, brothers, were brutally at the throats of each other, to their shame and that of the whole of Africa. They killed one another and left widows, orphans and widowers in large numbers. They demonstrated the words of Professor Patrick Loch Otieno Lumumba that in Africa the blood of ethnicity was thicker than the blood of nationalism. They wept and blamed the elites from both sides for playing the card of ethnicity rather than that of nationalism. They said they would not cooperate anymore with the selfish elites. The economy was bad. The people were not happy at all.

"These must be comforted, Nelson."

"Yes, Lord. The LORD has the grace, the peace, the comfort and He is Love. It is on Him we depend for everything."

"Nelson, time is running out. We must leave here and now. This place is very pathetic."

"I understand, Lord. It is, indeed."

"The people are crying, asking for when God will deliver them from the atrocities of the elites."

"Lord, who will stand during God's fair judgment? None! He is compassionate and merciful. Show mercy, LORD, I pray thee. We need the elites among us but let them be patriotic," Nelson pleaded.

"To where do we go now, Lord?"

"To River Moulouya in Morocco, the land of our friend, and the great patriot, late Ahmad Youssef."

"Okay, Lord," Nelson responded, wishing Youssef was alive so that he could meet him. He had wished to be there when Ahmad was being interred and possibly go to Atlantic Ocean to imagine how enslaved Africans, mostly from West Africa, were ferried through it to unknown lands, separated from their loved ones to be dehumanized in capitalist labour. He really wanted to stand by the Atlantic Ocean to have an imaginary feel of that unfortunate epoch.

***

"Here is Moulouya River in Morocco."

Without waiting to be asked by the angel, Nelson began to mumble between sobs. "Lord, I can see a multitude, very sad and weeping. They are still suffering from the effects and the aftermath of the Arab spring. They are crying, craving democratic government though not so sure if it will pay better than the ones they now have. Lord, let us move away from here, it is pathetic, I am weak. I can't stand this long."

"They initially wanted to gather at the Atlantic Coast at Casablanca and Rabat to weep but later changed their minds. They said the weeping there will be inconsolable as they could easily remember the ferrying of Africans through it to the plantations of the West and the bones of those that died and were thrown into the Ocean."

"I wouldn't have gotten over the sight, Lord!"

"With God by your side, you will. His grace will be sufficient for you. Do you want to see the birth place of Ahmad Youssef?"

"Oh! The LORD is good. He knows how to satisfy the desires of the righteous. I want to!" The angel took him there.

***

"This is the birth place of Ahmad Youssef. It is called El Jadida," the angel said to Nelson.

"Oh, El Jadida, how blessed are you to have given to Africa a worthy son in the person of Ahmad Youssef. We thank you. Remain blessed."

The angel took him to a graveyard.

"This is the tomb of Ahmad Youssef," the angel said.

"My mentor, great Youssef, continue to lie in peace. The heavens have noted with pleasure your love for Africa."

From there, the angel took him to the Atlantic Ocean.

***

"Lord what is this expanse of water. I can't see the end of it."

"This is the Atlantic Ocean."

"Woe to this Ocean, Lord! It enabled the ferrying of Africans to the West for slavery," Nelson cried, yet admiring the sight of cruising ships on the ocean, most of them passenger liners. He hoped to see *Queen Mary* and *Queen Elizabeth,* the two largest passenger ships in the world, one day. During a conference he attended some time ago in Kenya, he was told about them by an Egyptian who was a sailor but had died in a crash few years ago while flying over a mountainous region in one of the European countries. The black box analysis showed that an explosive device was detonated in the aircraft when it was flying at an altitude of 11,000 metres, heading 38 degrees, almost half way into the flight of 5,400 kilometres. The time remaining to get to their destination was 02.50 hours.

"Nelson, don't be emotional. The Atlantic Ocean is innocent. God created it for positive gains not for despicable acts by man. Even this Ocean wept for the slaves. It was not happy receiving the remains of some of them that died during the dark period."

"I see."

"Yes, many corpses of slaves were thrown out of the Ocean to the shore by great tidal waves to show that the Ocean was not happy."

"I am sorry for that, Lord."

"I am happy that you don't remember these things with malice for the West anymore. You want forgiveness and reconciliation. That is the way of God."

"Thank you, Lord."

"Both the blacks and the whites are God's creations. Ridiculing or dehumanizing people of whatever race is evil. God will not continue to tolerate this. Just wait and see. But Africa must wake up and progress. There is no need of sitting and fretting over the past. It has happened already and passed."

"What can Africans do? We should forgive the whites," Nelson maintained.

"Now, we are leaving to Nigeria, your country. We are going to Lokoja at the confluence of River Niger and its major tributary, the Benue River. Their sources are from Guinea and Northern Cameroon respectively. The River Niger empties into the Gulf of Guinea. Do you know Geography?"

"How do you know this geography, Lord?"

"Don't be funny, Nelson. Who created the earth? Is it not God? Am I not His angel who should know this? Men just know a little about it and yet they are so boastful."

"Sorry, Lord."

"Let us go."

***

"What do you see, Nelson," the angel asked while they were already at Lokoja.

"A great number of people wailing as in other places we have toured."

"Yes, they are crying because of the insecurity in the country. They are crying because there is so much injustice and corruption in the country. The money from oil has not change their lives significantly. There is fear everywhere."

"I know, Lord. I am a Nigerian."

"Nelson, God is specifically annoyed with Nigeria. She has not shown leadership qualities to other African countries. They look up to her for continental leadership but she has failed. She must wake up and lead Africa to dignified heights of political, technological and economic achievements against the ridicule of the world. But she must stop tribal, ethnic, religious, zonal and regional segregation to move ahead."

"Yes, Lord."

"Nelson, look at the waters of these two rivers, River Niger and River Benue, before the confluence. What do you notice?"

He looked but could not say anything."

"Look, their colours are different. The water of River Niger is turbid and cloudy because of its long journey through desert terrains, and that of the Benue River is a bit dark because of its fairly high organic content. After the confluence, they unite to give another colour like a mixed-blood."

"Lord, I know you have something to say on this. Let me listen to you, Lord."

"You are right. Presently, like the different colours of the waters from the two rivers, Africans are of two social statuses, rich and poor."

"I am listening, Lord."

"And as the waters come together at the confluence to be one, the LORD is going to bring together and integrate the rich and the poor together to a fair degree, thereby comforting the wailers. However, the honest, the patriotic and the hardworking people will still stand out in the crowd and shine like the stars in the sky or as a shooting star. God will do this justly."

"The LORD of justice, His ways are righteous. Let His perfect will be done," Nelson responded.

"Yes, He is going to do it through the rising patriots."

"Yes Lord." Nelson said, his face bright and cheerful.

"When that time comes, the needful and the basic necessities of life that the rich people have, the poor will also have; the food the rich people eat, the poor will eat and their children will walk shoulder to shoulder with one another. There will be fair redistribution of wealth and satisfaction of needs."

"The LORD of justice, the LORD of justice," Nelson praised God.

"When people unite and do justice, the LORD bestows His blessings upon their land. Yes, during that period, the manufacturing sector of the economy will blossom all over Africa."

"Thank you, Lord. I am happy to hear this from you."

"For now, go and rest. I will tell you the meaning of the other vision. Don't ask me when for God does things at His appointed time."

Nelson nodded in reverence. He was pleased with God's doings and appreciated the opportunity to be chosen by God. He appreciated God and the Angel and departed happier and more hopeful than ever.

EIGHT

ജ്ര

Nelson was sitting alone across the river which flowed through the forest in the west of Pa. He leaned on the same tree that the dove Matthew chased, settled down on. He meditated on his encounter with the angel on the visionary tour over some water bodies of some African countries. He thought of the gloomy Africans they saw during the tour, and how God had planned to comfort them; how the brooks of tears on their faces will be replaced with ripples of joy.

He stood up and moved to the river. Tadpoles were swimming playfully in the water. He picked a little stone and flicked it inside the water causing enduring ripples in the river as the stone landed. Nelson had learned some lessons from the happy lives of the tadpoles and the ripples. He wished a time would come when ripples of patriotism would be seen all over Africa and Africans would move happily like the tadpoles without any disturbance.

Nelson moved downstream the river. He came to a still pond which was almost surrounded by stones and sand. Never had there been a year, even during dry seasons, that water dried up in the pond; it was always filled to the brim. He saw fishes rambling around with gusto. He picked two stones and threw one into the pond. The fishes scattered. The water got settled a little while but not the fishes which have only returned in *handfuls* swimming around cautiously. Nelson threw in the second stone, scattering the fishes once again; only for them to return again in lesser numbers and more fearful.

As he stood ruminating over his observation, he reasoned that that was how Africa was quiet and peaceful before the 'stone' of slavery was thrown into her and she scattered, reducing her population. Africans tried to regain her peace after being hit by the 'stone' of slavery, another 'stone', the second 'stone', the 'stone' of colonialism, was thrown into her bosom and she became mentally destabilized; erroneously believing that she was inferior to other races. Nelson remembered that there was the third 'stone' that had been and was still being thrown into Africa; this 'stone' is the 'stone' of neo-colonialism. The first two were now physically passive but mentally active on the psyche of most Africans which ought not to be. But the third 'stone', the 'stone' of neo-colonialism, which was still being thrown into Africa, must be dealt with.

Nelson sighed while thinking that the three 'stones' should be eliminated completely to allow the unity of all nations for peace to reign. He said that this must be a mission for every global patriot, believing the world must be united.

Nelson returned to the dry tree and sat on its bark, resting his back against it. It was already noon. The sun shined directly on his head, drops of sweat cascading down his face from his forehead, wetting his shirt. He wiped the sweat off his face at regular intervals with the edge of his shirt. While sitting there, he fell into a trance in which he saw a gathering of Africans weeping because of injustice. He awoke, with a gloomy countenance.

"Nelson, what is on your mind?" the angel appeared, asking.

"Lord, how can the weepers and mourners be comforted? What is their hope?"

"Do not be faithless. Have you forgotten about the rising African patriots?"

"Sorry, Lord," he said, his face collapsing in shame. How could he have forgotten the vision or doubted the reality of the vision he had seen earlier on?

"Come, I will take you now on tour of some African countries as examples. You will see how God is going to bring glory to Africa," the angel said, grasping Nelson by the hand and off they went, starting from Ghana.

***

"Here is Mount Afadjoto in Ghana with a height of 885m (2,904ft)" the angel introduced.

They were at the foot of the Mount.

"Mount Afadjoto in Akwapim-Togo Ranges?" Nelson asked, his face carpeted in surprise for he had read about it in a geography text book.

"Yes, what do you see on its top?"

"A cluster of light," Nelson said, turning his eyes away; the light was so bright, it could blind the eyes.

As they spoke, a snake wriggled from the shrubs around in the realm of the spirit; it was trailing a toad but on noticing their spiritual presence, it raised its head while blowing up its neck in preparation to bite. Nelson was scared to the bones and wanted to run. A spiritual warfare!

"Where do you think you can run to, Nelson? Don't you trust God, the creator of everything?"

"I am sorry, my blessed one," his voice shaking.

Turning to the snake, the angel commanded it to die. It instantly did! "Nelson, no snake will appear again until we leave this place."

"Okay, my Lord,"

He raised his head and squinted his eyes to catch a glimpse of the cluster of light at the hilltop. The light sparkled gloriously.

"Nelson, the way I have dealt with this snake and made this place peaceful, so shall the rising African patriots bring political peace and economic development to Africa. Africans will rejoice greatly because the rising patriots will reconcile all classes of people to love one another selflessly."

"The LORD is able. All forces are under His control— the wind, the storm, the tidal waves…obey Him."

The angel shook his head and sighed heavily. The sigh was different from that of mortals; it was divine and consuming. It was necessitated by the sight of the weeping Ghanaians at the Volta River. The people were now raising their voices higher. The old men and women were now in ashes and torn clothes, weeping and rolling on the ground. They had declared a fast to seek the face of God for the healing of the land; much blood had been shed on the land especially during revolutions. They cried out, saying that they needed to see more significant economic changes in the lives of ordinary Ghanaians because Ghana was the land of gold. Such scenes of escalating weeping were almost all over Africa.

"Lord, may I ask why you shook your head and sighed," Nelson asked, curiously.

"What I am seeing has been hidden from you. It's the vision of the weeping Ghanaians at the Volta River. The site is becoming more pathetic."

"Give me the vision of that site again, Lord," Nelson pleaded, almost dejected.

"No more of that scene for you, Nelson. That vision will not be given to you again," the angel said.

"Whatever your decision is, it is good Lord. You know the best for me for God makes no mistakes."

"If all the people of the earth will understand this, as you do, they will not set up their will against God's will. God's will is life, theirs is death. They prefer death; and they will die."

"No Lord! Mercy, mercy is your way."

"For how long shall God be merciful to humanity?"

"Lord, Lord, if God will deal with us according to our ways, no one will live. No, Lord, that is not His nature. He is light and life."

"God has made available everything necessary for the survival of all men. This massive and selfish accumulation of wealth by man is primitive and causes misery all over the world. That is not God's design, Nelson."

"I know, Lord. Man is foolish. He does not know the way of peace. May the LORD put in us a new spirit to change our ways"

"God has given man freedom of choice; the will to choose. What has He not done for man, Nelson?"

"Lord! Lord! The clusters of lights are becoming many!" Nelson exclaimed, excited but yet to understand their meaning.

"You will see more of this," the angel said taking Nelson away to another place.

***

"Where are we now, Lord?" Nelson asked the angel.

"We are at Mount Njesuthi in the Drakensberg Mountains Range of South Africa. Have you heard of Mount Njesuthi?"

"No! Lord."

"What do you see, Nelson?"

"Pockets of bright light shining all over it," Nelson answered, feeling peaceful in his soul; he wondered where it came from. It was divine, the peace that knew no bound and felt by patriots anywhere in the world; its source is LOVE.The Christians say God is Love, and so it is the peace the LORD gives which He had been calling people to but man is unheeding. Some persons died yesterday; others will die today, some still yet will die tomorrow. No dead person had ever been reported to take his amassed material wealth to the world beyond and yet, man refuses to understand and he won't understand; vain glory, vain glory, was sweeping the earth with great casualties.

"Nelson, the light you are seeing shall overpower all acts of darkness to bring enduring political and economic progress to Africa."

"But Lord, what is this light?"

"Don't be in a hurry. You shall be told at the appointed time."

"Okay, Lord."

***

"Nelson, we have left South Africa long ago, can you tell me where we are now?" the angel asked. He couldn't wait for an answer.

"Nelson, we are at Volcan Karisimi in the Virunga Mountains, north-eastern Rwanda. What can you see?"

"Pockets of light from the top down to the foot of the mountain," Nelson answered, admiring the points of the light on the top of the snowcapped volcano and the ones interspersed among the trees of the rainforest at its side. Gorillas were seen roaming the surrounding highlands. Two of them were fighting, destroying shrubs around.

"Lord, can a future volcanic activity be expected again in this place?"

"Who told you that there was a Volcano here?"

"It was my Geography teacher, many years ago, when I was in the secondary school."

The angel could not go further on this but said, "There will be surges of spiritual volcano that will sweep away only wickedness (not the wicked for He will reform them. He only hates the wickedness in them. He created all for good).

NINE

ꟷ

"I will not be able to do this, Lord," Matthew complained.

He spoke in a dream after being informed by the angel of the LORD that he would succeed Nelson Mamman to keep the torch of the campaign for patriotism shining in Africa. The day was hot and dry, and Matthew was resting outside the garden, thinking of the kind of zeal that Nelson Mamman showed when he fell asleep and the dream came.

***

Nelson and Mercy, his wife, had gone to the farm when the angel told Matthew in the garden that he would succeed Nelson. The farm looked well attended to. The Nelsons maintained it adequately and it was fertile, yielding so much every year like that of the wine district of the Western Cape Province in

South Africa where Africans laboured for whites during apartheid for paltry wages. Remunerations were also manipulated to ensure perpetual dependence of black labourers to whites, and to prevent economic empowerment of the Africans. Nelson felt hurt anytime he remembered the mean systems. That day in the farm, he recalled and he contorted his face in horrific aversion. He hissed and tried dispelling the painful recollection, trying so much to not hate.

"Mine, what made you hiss?" Mercy asked as they were working on the farm. She would always insist on knowing what troubled her husband. She knew how to use her looks, gestures, voice and actions for her husband's therapy. In the village, people knew her for that. She was an epitome of beauty and she submitted wholly to her husband in the typical African tradition which abhorred the distorted notion of gender equality that was threatening the peace of many homes and escalating the rate of marital divorce all over the world.

"Don't worry, Mine. I am just fine." She did not believe him. However, she decided not to press on. She knew when to do so. She had studied her husband well.

***

"Matthew, you will surely succeed Nelson on this project of ensuring that patriotism is entrenched in Africa," the angel insisted.

"I am not a man of letters, you know this, my blessed one," Matthew would not stop complaining.

"The spirit that is in Nelson will indwell you and make you perform excellently. The LORD will help you."

"Oh, the blessed one, can't you just leave me alone? You should understand me, please."

"How can I understand when you are setting up your will against the LORD's? You must decide now who is to be honoured between the two of you."

"Must you go to that extent? Who am I to stand in the place of God? I am but grass, dust, ash and nothing more before Him, our Maker."

"That is right. Therefore, don't argue anymore with me on this divinely concluded matter."

"Let the will of the LORD be done in my life," Matthew succumbed, wondering if he could be as charismatic as Nelson. He has great potentials in him but he was yet to believe that and to put them to effect.

"Matthew, Nelson will soon return home."

"Yes, it is almost time for him to return from the farm."

"Oh you man of little understanding!"

"What is it, the blessed one?"

"Do you want me to come plain before you understand what I mean by Nelson will soon return home?"

Matthew quickly understood what the angel meant by *"Nelson will soon return home."* He will soon die. He began to weep.

"Stop weeping! This worthy son of Africa has done greatly for Africa. He has fought gallantly against all forms of selfishness in Africa. It is time for him to rest."

"The blessed one, will the heavens celebrate his death like that of Ahmed Youssef, the Moroccan?" Matthew asked, believing Nelson worthy of such honour.

"There is no man that has humanity at heart that will not be honoured by the heavens when he passes on. It is a thing of joy in heaven to have fruitful achievers return back home. It is always like that."

"I am pleased to hear this from you. Nelson is worthy of that; he is worthy."

"So prepare to take over from where Nelson stops. That is why you were made to take part in Nelson's activities under God's divine arrangement. You have represented him in conferences where you delivered papers. Can you remember how you were praised for the paper you presented in South Africa sometime ago under the topic, PATRIOTISM: THE PATHWAY TO NATION BUILDING? Many people took note of you, saying you are an orator with a blatant streak for patriotism which is a quality of a good leader. You will lead other African patriots on patriotic campaign."

"May the LORD help me," Matthew said and sighed heavily.

"He will," the angel responded, telling Matthew that the rising African patriots, unlike most African leaders, would groom patriotic successors with no bias as Nelson had done to him. They would groom successors for the good of Africa and not for selfish reasons.

The absence of mentorship for good people that would take over the future of Africa caused underdevelopment in the continent.

***

On the day the angel appeared to Matthew, he also appeared to Nelson in a vision. He repeated the vision of the cluster of light points he had shown him in different parts of Africa.

"The blessed one, this vision, again?" Nelson asked.

"Yes; you asked for the meaning of the points of the light. Didn't you?"

"I did."

"You've known the meaning."

"I have not, the blessed one."

"The rising African patriots radiating in a glow in the horizon will fill Africa as these clusters of light. The people you saw in the vision are coming to do business in Africa because it will become a beehive of economic activities."

"Oh, the ways of the LORD are mysterious. Who can understand them?"

"The man who loves justice can. The LORD is just. Do you understand?" the angel added.

"Yes, I do," Nelson answered, excited to know that Africa would regain her glory lost from the days of slavery and colonialism. The loss had been sustained by neo-colonialism and by the activities of some unpatriotic Africans. But his joy was short lived as the angel revealed to him that he shall soon return home.

"Nelson, my friend, I have told you that you will not be here when the rising patriots manifest. Go and put your house in order for you will soon join your mentor, Ahmad Youssef," the angel said with an air of finality, looking at Nelson deep in the eye.

The angel passed the news coolly without a slight betrayal of emotion from his countenance. Why should he worry? The angel knew that God as a potter breaks and remolds His works as He wishes. No one dares ask Him why He does so.

Nelson's eyes welled up with tears. Tried as he might he couldn't control his emotions. He was sad over the campaign for patriotism in Africa he would be leaving behind, wondering whether Matthew whom he had groomed and exposed to some international limelight will be effective for the job.

"Nelson, I know why you are worried. Don't be discouraged. Matthew has not been with you all these years for nothing. God divinely arranged for him to be your friend to ready him for this moment. Don't you believe that you have adequately groomed him for this work?"

"May the name of the LORD be honoured. He can do the work. May the LORD empower him doubly and even more to succeed," he prayed, remembering how he had been receiving commendation on Matthew's leadership qualities.

"The LORD will be with him and cause him to succeed," the angel assured.

***

A week later, the angel appeared to Nelson in sleep, reminding him of his impending death. He would die while sleeping. The angel said.

***

One night while Nelson was sleeping, his lips parted, exposing his teeth in a wide grin even as he slept. His wife was amazed at this strangeness.

"Mine, why are you laughing?" Mercy asked, tapping him on his back.

"Oh, Mine, you have disturbed me. I was in a heavenly realm, a realm that is above the enticement of this troubled earth. Don't bring me back again into this flesh, this container, please," Nelson said before falling asleep again. He snored and started laughing again, calling Ahmad Youssef. Mercy would not allow this dream to end by itself. She tapped him again.

"Mine, did you not hear what I told you? I told you not to wake me up again. I am at peace with myself."

"You're dreaming, Mine! You've been calling Ahmad Youssef! What is wrong with you?"

"Whether it is a dream or a reality, all I know is that I have never been this peaceful, never been this serene."

"Tell me about the dream," Mercy demanded, looking sad and confused.

"I saw myself discussing with Ahmad Youssef in a beautiful place with golden streets and streams of living water. The people there, I have never seen anything joyful. It is a glorious place to be."

"Apart from Ahmad Youssef, you said you saw other people," Mercy said, surprised.

"Yes, many people. Among them were African patriots that passed on many years ago. Mine, I love the place."

"Mine, we need to pray about this dream."

"Are you afraid?"

"Yes, we don't know its meaning. It could be good or bad omen. We can't say. Only God can."

"Yes, you are correct. You are a virtuous woman."

Mercy prayed that God may avert any ill omen the dream could have and if it was a good thing coming their way, she prayed it might be fulfilled. Nelson answered amen, hoping that it was patriotism that was coming to water Africa and beyond her borders. He had always been selfless. He had not changed.

It was his wish that the whole world would enjoy real life. He knew that to really live was to care for one another not minding regional, national, racial and religious differences. He would never trade off this virtue for anything. Yes, slavery, colonialism, nepotism, racism, segregation, selfishness, hatred, neo-colonialism and the likes debase man. The perpetrators of these social ills, whites or blacks, should change. If not because of the mercy of the LORD, the perpetrators and their facilitators would have long been consumed; even those who ought to speak against these evils but still kept silent would not have been spared.

***

It had been a cloudy day. People expected downpour since morning but the cloud would not let go of the rains. Matthew wanted to go to Kaduna to buy some history books but had to wait for the rain to fall before setting out. He was looking up in the sky at regular intervals observing the sky for any sign of rain. The cloud was so thick, the village blurry but still the rain did not come. Thunders rumbled in echoes over the village and windstorms hummed briskly past thatched roofs and mud bricks. The sky was sullen, the atmosphere dull, dull as when the thunders and the windstorms of slavery and colonialism ravaged Africa and stripped her of her ancient civilizations that used to be more sophisticated than the West's. Similarly, the thunders and windstorms of un-patriotism were ravaging Africa; holding it down in deplorable squalor.

***

With the atmosphere still cloudy, Matthew quickened his pace to the pond, the same place he went to see Nelson in his reverie.

Frogs croak hoarsely, scared of the dimness of the atmosphere. Some were leaping into the pond from its banks. Some even attempted coming out but held back due to the scary weather.

While Matthew was concentrating on the frogs, the angel of the LORD said to him, "Matthew, move over and stand where you stood with Nelson the day when you couldn't see the vision he saw. The LORD is going to crown you prince of patriotism with the same vision," the angel spoke audibly and gently. Matthew obeyed.

"Raise your head and look at the direction Nelson had asked you to look at the other time and tell me what you see."

"The blessed one, I can barely see in this cloudy atmosphere, it is dark all over the place."

The angel was not pleased for Matthew had little faith. He didn't know that God could intervene by even subverting the law of nature. That is a miracle; what Christians always yearn for; even Muslims and other faiths. Some days, desperate enough, Nelson prayed for a miracle that Africans may be patriotic. Another day he prayed for a miracle to eradicate racism all over the world. But God works His miracles as at when He likes.

"The LORD is God, the Alpha and the Omega, the creator of everything. The forces of nature do His biddings. If you persist in your unbelief, you will die. Now, look up as I have instructed," the angel spoke firmly. Matthew had no option but to obey. Only stony hearts will want to go against God and die.

"What do you see?"

"I can see a cloud of infants with brooms in their hands and a very big canopy hovering over them, elevating. They had great enthusiasm and joy sparkles over their face."

"That is what Nelson wanted you to see the other day you met him here but you were unable to for by then you lacked patriotism for Africa. Now you can see; God has opened your eyes."

"These are the rising African patriots that Nelson has been seeing?"

"Yes, they are. As from today, you are commissioned to put on the shoes of Nelson for this project of patriotism. In your days, the rising African patriots will physically manifest."

"Let the will of the LORD be done. The brooms in their hands and the big umbrella over them; what are they for?"

"The brooms will be used to sweep out all forms of bad politics and economy in Africa. The umbrella will cover all Africans against the recurrence of these ills again. Africa's lost glory will be restored. God has spoken and so shall it be. He is not a man that He should lie."

Matthew wanted to bow down and worship. The angel prevented him saying, "If you will sincerely preach the gospel of patriotism and live it, that enough is worship to God."

"Okay, the blessed one," Matthew conceded.

"Go back to your house. It is the Spirit of the LORD that led you here to show you the vision. But don't go to Kaduna for the books. Aminu Suleiman, the bookseller, has gone to Niger Republic on a business trip. He will be back next week."

"Let the LORD, the omniscience, be honoured; He knows everyone and his activities," Matthew said as he trekked back home.

***

After some days Nelson had a dream in which he met Ahmad Youssef, he knew it was time he prepared his house as God asked him to.

***

One day, after cautioning his family to love and fear God in all their doings, he read out the words of James Allen to them.

"Dwell constantly in mind upon eternal justice, the eternal good. Endeavour to lift yourself above the personal and the transitory into the impersonal and permanent. Shake off the delusion that you are being injured or oppressed by another, and try to realize, by a profounder comprehension of your inner life and the laws that govern that life, that you are only really injured by what is within you.

"There is no practice more degrading, debasing, and soul-destroying than that of self-pity. Cast it out from you. While such a canker is feeding upon your heart, you can never expect to grow into a fuller life. Cease from the condemnation of others, and begin to condemn yourself. Condone none of your acts, desires, or thoughts that will not bear comparison with spotless purity or endure the light of sinless good. By so doing, you will be building your house upon the rock of the Eternal, and all that is

required for your happiness and well-being will come to you in its own time."[1]

Nelson also read the following words also written by James Allen with explanation to the family.

"Your true wealth is your stock of virtue, and your true power the uses to which you put it. Rectify your heart and you will rectify your life. Lust, hatred, anger, vanity, pride, covetousness, self-indulgence, self-seeking, obstinacy – all these are poverty and weakness; whereas love, purity, gentleness, meekness, patience, compassion, generosity, self-forgetfulness, and self-renunciation – all these are wealth and power."[2]

"Mine," Nelson called. "The children might not really have gotten the message of James Allen. You'll have to explain to them when they come of age."

His wife cut in immediately he gave his message.

"What are you saying? Won't you be around? I can't really understand the things you say lately. You mean..." she sighed and continued, "No! You mean.... I am upset. Are you dying soon?"

"Mine, gather your emotions together. A man will occasionally counsel his family in this manner. Our lives are in the hands of God and... and, anyway it's n-no-thing," he stuttered.

"And what?" Mercy demanded, becoming more baffled than ever, imagining a life without Nelson, the man she had spent her life with and truly loved; lonely it would be.

"Teach the children to be patriotic in all they do. They must join the rising African patriots when they eventually come to make Africa great and...

and…and I want…where is Matthew? Tell him…," He stuttered again and remained silent.

That night, Nelson died peacefully in his sleep, his face revealing a thin smile and his body still warm.

Mercy and the children wailed and wept, their voices echoing through the village. Nobody could comfort them but God.

***

One night as she got too tired of crying, she slept off in the couch and had this dream of an angel calling her to be patient and comforted. The angel told her that her husband was in heaven, joyful and wanting to let her and the children know how much he was doing well. For his patriotism and feats while on earth, heaven celebrated his return home. Thus, she and the children should be happy for their father was somewhere sublime, resting in peace.

***

The night that Nelson passed away, a comet traversed the heavens and the stars dimmed their light. There was a partial eclipse of the moon. The following day, the heat from the sun, though there were no clouds, was moderate and comforting, the atmosphere unusually sober. Even the atmosphere and the heavens celebrated Nelson's return home.

***

Matthew was away in Abuja when Nelson died. The death was revealed to him that night by God. He saw a vision where he was with Nelson at the bank of River Wild, both weeping for the world's troubles. They wept bitterly remembering what they had learned from the book, *How Europe Underdeveloped Africa,* by Walter Rodney. The scene was like that of the children of Israel by the rivers of Babylon, wailing when they remembered Zion, the City of God. They wept for Africa's lost glory and history.

As Nelson and Matthew were weeping, an angel of the LORD appeared, looking graceful and admirable. He threaded softly towards Nelson and collected a sort of a flash light, handing it over to Matthew. The angel took Nelson across the river to the opposite bank. They walked away and disappeared into the cloud, leaving Matthew frightened and stunned.

Matthew realized the flash light taken from Nelson and given to him was the flash light for the campaign for patriotism in Africa. He had been told that he would succeed Nelson. It had been confirmed now. He must start work immediately after Nelson's funeral. He was determined to show a good example of what he taught people. He recalled a popular saying of Mahatma Gandhi: *"You must be the change you wish to see in the world."*

He would not do otherwise if he were to lead and be revered by his followers. That was a noble assignment, a divine one and he made up his mind to succeed at it with the help of God.

***

Nelson's death was featured in one of the African weekly magazine based in Eritrea. The news reads:

Another African patriotic icon, in the person of Nelson Mamman, with a yearning to see global brotherhood of all mankind, has passed on yesterday in the night in his humble village of Pa, Kagarko Local Government Area of Kaduna State, Nigeria.
News of his death, as posted to us by our Kaduna based correspondent, says that he died, hoping that patriotism would one day be firmly enshrined in the hearts of Africans for the progress of Africa. We, of the Continental Africa Development Watch, are convinced that he died also hoping that the West will one day attain real freedom, the freedom of the conscience, from the moral monster called racism which has violated the dignity of man and the unity of mankind. We are so convinced of this opinion because his recent intercontinental activities on universal patriotism are known to all, the progressives and the un-progressives. It is therefore a moral burden on us, in line with the core values of our company which include patriotism, to call the West to embrace true freedom, the freedom of conscience, by dealing once and for all with the issue of racism in all its ramifications. Africans must arise now, along with other nations of the world, to make Africa and the world a better place

where the sense of equity and justice shall reign supreme in our hearts. This will make globalization acceptable by all since it will be all inclusive.

In conclusion, the remains of Nelson Mamman shall be laid to rest on Thursday of the coming week. Details of the funeral shall be unfolded to the public very soon.

For now, let all patriotic Africans accept our condolence.

TEN

ꕥ

Matthew returned from Abuja to Pa Village having been informed by Titi, his wife, of Nelson's death. On his way back, he stopped at Kasuwa Dole, a yam market along Kaduna- Abuja express way. He purchased some tubers of yam he would use to feed mourners that would come to console him over Nelson's death. In the market, three revenue collectors were quarrelling with a man who refused to pay tax on yams he sold in the market. He intervened for peace to reign and advised the man to be patriotic and pay the tax, saying government revenue was what was used for developing a nation. The man agreed to pay his tax and Matthew even started orientating people on patriotism.

Abuja to Pa was an hour drive but it seemed shorter for Matthew that day. He was so engrossed in thoughts of Nelson's death. His mind wandered between the death and his commissioning into the vacant position left by Nelson. It was a demanding task and he knew for he had seen how much Nelson toiled before he died. However, he was determined to do the same.

"*Let your mind be still, Matthew. God will always be there for you. Africa is already pregnant with patriotism, waiting to be given birth,*" a voice within him muttered.

"The blessed one," He knew it was an angel speaking to him, "how can I comfort Mercy on the death of her husband? You know how close they were."

"Do you have any comfort or peace to give, Matthew?" the angel asked.

"No, the blessed one," he responded.

"The LORD is our comfort, the peace, the hope, the guide, the security, the provider and the protector of all men. He has comforted her even before the death of her husband. When you get home, you will see what I'm talking of."

"The LORD is the hope of Africa; only a foolish man doubts Him. He is worthy of praise," Matthew agreed, remembering a sermon he heard two years ago. The preacher said that only men who fear God have inner peace.

That sermon, preached by Pastor K. Iku, had elements of patriotism. He called on people to love one another, love God and their countries to make the world a better place. Pastor Iku, a bearded and well-built man with a stout structure was little less like the biblical Goliath. He died some years ago and Matthew attended the funeral service. He cried sneakily as he remembers how kind and patriotic Pastor Iku was. He immediately wiped the tears off his face so passengers wouldn't notice him.

"Blessed one; let me ask one more question".

"You can," the angel responded, his voice accommodating.

"How will the West be delivered from the evil of racism? Since slavery, many blacks have been lynched; now political and economic lynching is orchestrated against Africa and some developing countries. God should mediate."

"Hold your peace, Matthew. As the rising African patriots are coming, the LORD shall raise progressives in the West to sweep racism away. The events are blossoming already."

"May the LORD be honoured."

"For now, as soon as you get home, you eat and go straight to Nelson's house."

"Okay, blessed one."

***

"Matthew, your friend is gone; your friend is gone. Before he died, he spoke about patriotism and asked of you. You know how patriotism occupied his mind while he lived," Mercy said immediately she set her eyes on Matthew as he entered the compound.

"I know that very well, Mercy. Take heart," Matthew responded. He struggled to stop the tears welling up in his eyes.

"It is okay, Matthew. I am consoled with the fact that my husband died thinking of a patriotic Africa, and praying for the West to be free from racism. He died a patriot. Actually, patriots never die."

"Yes, they do not. They are immortalized in the hearts of the people from one generation to another."

"Yes, I'm sure my husband will be a patriotic monument in the hearts of the progressives all over the world."

"An indomitable monument for that matter," Matthew added.

"Tell the people not to weep for my husband; let them weep for themselves, their children and for Africa and then for the West which is enslaved by racial prejudices," Mercy said, looking into the sky as if she was watching the spirit of Nelson ascending the heavens. She abruptly jerked herself back to life.

"Did you hear me, Matthew?" she asked while waving at no one and staring at the sky as if she was saying goodbye to the spirit of Nelson.

"Yes, I do," Matthew mumbled, his face lacking colour as he meditated over Mercy's utterances.

"They are," Mercy continued, "to weep for themselves, their children and Africa by being patriotic. They are to also pray so the West can be free of prejudice. This will rest my husband's spirit."

Matthew was not surprised by Mercy's show of courage, for the angel told him that she had been consoled.

***

Nelson's funeral was on a Thursday, two weeks after his death. Enough time was given for his death to be publicized for he was nationally and internationally acclaimed. Some progressive groups in the West had started noting his philosophy on patriotism and racism. Even obstinate racists had started loosening up. In the West, brothers were rising against brothers; friends against friends; parents against children; spouses against spouses, and workers against workers for the evil of racism haunted them. A new dawn of brotherhood all across the world will soon emerge. Social stratification and racial prejudice was about to be conquered and dispelled.

An extract from an editorial of a London based newspaper, *Patriotism and Development*, said this on Nelson's funeral:

"…. Having analyzed with unusual admiration the exploits of this patriotic son of Africa, Mr. Nelson Mamman, whose remains shall be committed to mother earth tomorrow, we wish to call on our brothers and sisters in the West to do away with the false notion of superiority as embodied in racism and face the fact that all human beings, no matter where they come from, are dignified creations of God with His divine image fairly imbued in all. It is good for all men to think on these words of Apostle Paul to the Corinthians that "Now, brothers, I have applied these things to myself and Apollos for your benefit, so that you may learn from us the meaning of the saying, 'Do not go beyond what is written.' Then you will not take pride in one man over against another. For who makes you different from anyone else? What do you have that you did not receive? And if you did receive it, why do you boast as though you did not?"[1]. *Therefore, we must treat all people without violating the sense of equity and justice. In this way, the true peace that has been eluding the world will come to stay.*

"Therefore, we call on all Africans to be patriotic enough to resist vehemently any internal or external attempt to ravage their economies and destabilize their political structures. This is the sure

and the enduring way to honour the likes of Nelson Mandela, 'Nelson Mamman', and 'Ahmad Youssef'.

"In Conclusion, we, of the Patriotism and Development newspaper, during our recent management meeting, have decided to mount a voracious campaign against all forms of racial inclination till it is dismantled in totality."

***

By 10am, all groups of singers were already seated. The church Nelson attended in Pa village was not very spacious; it had capacity for only five hundred and thirty-one people. Thousands of people came for his funeral. As such, the funeral service was held in the open, in the vicinity of where he sat when he was given the vision of the rising African patriots. Pastor Micah Stephen, the resident pastor, gave the sermon that day.

"....What have we gathered here for? Are we gathered here to mourn the passing on of Nelson, the patriot? We must not mourn for him. He is to be celebrated for his spirit of patriotism. He must be celebrated for a life well-lived, a selfless life and a patriotic life. If we are to cry, we should cry for the advent of patriotism in our hearts for the progress of Africa. We should cry for true brotherhood of mankind. Let each and everyone here ask what he or she can do for the progress of Africa. Mo Ibrahim, Alhaji Aliko Dangote, Professor Patrick Loch Otieno Lumumba and others, although they are few, are already doing something in this regard. We cannot do something good for Africa unless we are patriotic like Nelson whose casket is presently laid before us. The best and enduring tribute we can give to this African

patriot, from now on, is to be patriotic in our thoughts, speeches and actions. Anything apart from this is inconsequential.

If the heavens are celebrating the passing on of Nelson, who are we, mere mortals, not to do the same. He is now resting in the bosom of the LORD," the pastor said, pursing his lips.

"As for you," he continued, *"the family of late Nelson, his name will open ways for you anywhere you go to in Africa and beyond for your father was renowned for international speeches on unity. And this privilege must not be abused, for you must protect this name by always observing his core value of patriotism. When you do this, you will build your reputation as your father did…."*

He was silent for some minutes as he looked at the congregation searchingly as if he was expecting someone to speak. The congregation waited to hear the next words of exhortation from him but he had concluded already and was making to pray for Nelson's family.

"Let the family of our beloved late father, brother and friend, come forward for prayer," Pastor Stephen said.

"Retired Pastor Pius Thomas, the Baptist Pastor, who has come to identify with us in this trying period, will say the prayer for the family."

Pastor Pius Thomas was from Liberia, the first independent African country, and also the first country in Africa to be governed by a democratically elected female President. His ancestors were slaves in the Americas. Pastor Thomas was so patriotic; he preached to his members during his active years as a Pastor. He also gave lectures at other secular gatherings. He never squandered the church's money. His members loved him for this and for his humility.

"God of glory; the God that has authority over all powers," Pastor Pius Thomas began, *"seen and unseen, known and unknown; the God that loves justice and love all men, black or white, without segregation; the God that hates racial prejudices; we thank you for this day, a day that we are burying our father, son, friend and patriot, Nelson. We thank you for his patriotic life. Help us to emulate him. As you liberated our forefathers from slavery and colonialism, LORD, liberate Africa from lack of patriotism and neo-colonialism. For the family of our dear brother, Nelson, his wife and children, comfort and keep them in peace. Let your peace reign in their hearts. Because of their late father, may your love never depart from them. For our brothers, the white men, give them a new heart to know that there is no racism in heaven so that they will be delivered from this social cancer enslaving them. LORD, you are good. Thank you for answered prayer. Amen."*

The congregation chorused a dull Amen and remained seated; no one was in a hurry to leave. They revered and admired Nelson; they wished they could live a life like his. But one thing they did not know was that; to be patriotic is not just a wish but a will. God has given man the freedom to choose the path he wants to thread but he will always face the consequences. Africans must choose the patriotic path to progress along with the West and the East and reject evil of social prejudices such as racism.

"Is there any announcement from the family members," Bulus Mallam, the service leader, shouted in a hoarse voice from the pulpit.

A man in his early forties came out to the pulpit.

"All protocols observed. I give honour to everyone here present with the honour God has given to him," the man began, smiling to the amazement of the people.

"This is time for celebrating my brother, Nelson. He lived well and made our family and Africa proud. I urge everyone to relax and thank God this day. I am assuring you that even Nelson's body in the casket is thanking God. Though he is dead, his face is smiling. That is a sign that he had lived a satisfactory life and we all know this. That is enough to comfort us in this trying moment and hereafter. But let me quickly add, we must all leave here after this funeral service, with the thought of letting patriotism reign in Africa and in any country we find ourselves in the world. We know Africans are not racists. Having said this, I have the following announcements to make. First of all, after the internment of our brother, all the clergy men shall take their refreshment in the church pastorium. Secondly, I was made to understand that people from Morocco, the country of Nelson's mentor, late Ahmad Youssef; people from Uganda (the pearl of Africa), South Sudan (presently the youngest independent African country) and South Africa (the rainbow nation) are here to encourage and mourn with us. They will take their refreshment at Matthew's house, a close friend to our late brother, Nelson. You all know him since he has represented Nelson in some international conferences on patriotism.

Thirdly, I pray God give us all understanding on this matter of patriotism epitomized by late Nelson.

Amen," the man concluded before stepping away from the pulpit.

"We shall be seated after the closing prayer. In going out, the pastors will be in the front, followed by the casket then the congregation. Let us be patient and obey this instruction," the service leader pleaded with his eyes rolling round the congregation.

***

".... Dust to dust, ash to ash...," Pastor Stephen pronounced, dropping brown soil on the casket which had been lowered into the sepulcher. Nelson's life was thus closed. The Pastor appointed one among the Ugandans to say the last prayer.

"Our father in heaven, thank you for this day. Thank you for the success of this funeral service. Help us to go from this graveyard and always remember our friend, Nelson, and his noble ideals and live by them. Thank you for the life of this patriot. Help all of us in Africa to be patriotic like him. Amen."

***

"Sheikh Faisal Ahmadu, what actually prompted you to attend this funeral service of Nelson Mamman?" a reporter from Ghana asked. The Sheikh had been a close associate of Pastor Micah Stephen.

"Who wouldn't respect even in death, a man of honour like Nelson? He was a patriot, indeed," he said.

"In this regard, what is your advice to Africans?"

"First of all, we must love Africa, our identity, our cultures and one another. This is the only way we can be patriotic."

"Sheikh, religious intolerance is one of the banes preventing the development of Africa. What can you sincerely say about this," the reporter continued, wishing the Sheikh continued to respond.

"Actually, this is a problem we all wish to eradicate. You know I have been preaching about religious tolerance. The resident Pastor of this church, who preached at this funeral service today, has also been preaching about it. I call all patriotic people to rise against religious intolerance. I call on the followers of the two major faiths to not be deceived anymore by politicians. We must move ahead."

"Do you have any other advice?"

The Sheikh thought for a moment. His face showed that he was groping his heart for words. He later spoke.

"The media should be active and help on these issues of lack of patriotism and religious intolerance. Patriotism must not be sacrificed on the altar of selfishness no matter what."

"Thank you so much, Sheikh Faisal."

"Thank you," the Sheikh responded, adjusting his white turban that seemed new and oversized, and turned to greet some people.

The reporter went on to Nelson's house to interview his wife, Mercy.

***

"Madam," the reporter called.

"You are very courageous even amidst mourning your late husband; can you tell me what your secret is?"

"The secret is that God has comforted me with the thought that my husband loved Africa by being patriotic. See the crowd of people, the rich and the poor, the mighty and the low, the Christians and the Muslims, all manner of people are gathered here to pay him their last respect. Nothing is more important than worshipping the living God, for one to live, love and die for one's country or continent," Mercy answered, immediately turning to speak with the team from South Africa.

"Sorry, madam, one more question, please," the reporter requested, realizing that he won't have Mercy's attention anymore because of the crowd.

"My friend, can't you just understand and let me be for now, please?" Mercy retorted.

"I do, madam. That was why I said 'one more question'. Just answer me, please," insisted the reporter.

"What is it?"

"With your husband now dead, how do you intend to spend the rest of your life?"

"Preaching patriotism; preaching patriotism and preaching patriotism, starting from Nigeria, and then all over Africa. Thank you," she said with finality and turned again to give attention to the South African team.

"Thank you, madam," the reporter said, satisfied. At least he was able to interview the widow of the great patriot; what a boost for his journalistic credentials.

"We are here to identify with you in this period of mourning which is not only for the patriots in Nigeria but for all the patriots in Africa. We assure you that we from South Africa, will return home to keep on preaching the gospel of patriotism," the leader of the South African team said.

The features of the South African team's leader were similar to that of the late Nelson Mandela of South Africa. It was as if he was deliberately chosen for people at the funeral to remember the late Nelson Mandela.

"You South Africans must not disappoint the spirit of my husband. He changed his named from Julius to Nelson in honour of Nelson Mandela because he admired him for his patriotism," Mercy said.

"We are very much aware of this with due admiration of your late husband's life. We will not disappoint him. To disappoint him is to disappoint and embarrass Africa."

"Thank you for coming. Have you been served?"

"Sure; thanks a lot," they chorused. This impressed Mercy and she wished Africans would be united like that with the spirit of patriotism against all odds. The Moroccan team was waiting. She paid attention to them,

"The people from the country of late Ahmad Youssef, the mentor to my late husband, you took the trouble to be here; thank you. That is so patriotic of you. You are welcome," Mercy said.

"We should be here. We are some of the disciples of late Ahmad Youssef. The mentor to your late husband is a household name in the homes of the progressives in Morocco. They send in their condolences. Be calm, be calm, the work of your husband and other patriotic Africans will be fruitful. This should comfort you," the spokesman for the team said.

"Thank you so much," Mercy responded. She told them of how her late husband was so fond of late Ahmad Youssef, hissing in remembrance of that and unable to prevent tears falling from her eyes; emotion had won over her courage this time.

Finally, the South Sudanese team moved to greet her.

"I thank you for coming. If you go back home, preach patriotism to aid what Mo Ibrahim is doing to entrench good governance in Africa. He is a patriot par excellence. All Africans must support him. You are welcome," she advised.

***

A week after the burial of Nelson Mamman, Mercy called her children and advised them to take after the character of their late father.

".... Finally, all I want from you is love of God and patriotism. These are the best things you can do in your schools, at home, in the bus and anywhere. Africa will be great. The whites will one day rush to stay in Africa. God will be with all of you," she concluded and blessed them and waited for future events on patriotism to come up.

ELEVEN

ꕥ

The visiting teams from Uganda, South Sudan, South Africa and Morocco had some discussions with Matthew on how to entrench a system of patriotism throughout Africa before they departed for their respective countries.They promised to carry out a vigorous campaign on patriotism that would cover the whole of Africa as soon as possible. It was during this discussion that Matthew told them how an angel had revealed to him as done to Nelson Mamman about the rising African patriots. They were excited. The visiting Moroccan team leader told them that late Ahmad Youssef was given such a vision before he died. This assured them the more of the good days that would soon come to Africa. They rejoiced exceedingly, looking forward to their emergence. With this, they concluded that their work of entrenching patriotism in Africa had been divinely undergirded. Therefore, they resolved to keep on calling Africans to straighten their paths for the coming of the African patriots. They agreed to organize a conference on the theme: AWAY WITH DECEPTION AND EGOITISM FOR PATRIOTISM IN AFRICA. They chose Matthew as the leader and Faisal Mohammed, a member of the Moroccan team, as the Secretary for the group of the patriots. They resolved to approach African Development Bank (AFDB) to sponsor the conference because they believed that patriotism was central to economic and developmental strides envisioned by the AFDB.

"I sincerely thank all of you for your love across national borders. This reminds me of the communal love that once existed in Africa before the evil of slave trade and colonialism visited and dispersed us to our artificial tents. We will gather again to unite our souls for the progress of Africa. Once again, accept my gratitude," Matthew concluded, embracing each and every one of them, saying with tears in his eyes '*Africa shall rise again.*'

He wished them safe flights to their respective countries.

***

Matthew fondly called his wife 'mommy' and the wife called him 'daddy'. Africans hardly call their spouses by their names. They would always adopt pet names for each other. Some shy spouses trying to avoid using romantic names for their spouses would call their spouses relating to the names of their children such as Baba Bulus (Bulus' father) or Mama Ibeji (Ibeji's mother). African culture values respect and dignity, and they are embedded in most customs and traditions.

"Daddy, you have been reading a lot these days. You read books on China, United States of America, Britain, Malaysia, Australia, Germany, France and other countries," Titi observed.

Unlike Mercy, she had bleached her skin and cherished western cultures. Matthew resolved to help her be liberated from this mental slavery. This was a task for him to achieve. She must be patriotic and love African cultures and customs just as he did. She was docile and he knew she would allow him help her throw away the shackles of such slavery— a slavery that belittled one and uplifted another. Actually, the West was not to be entirely blamed for this because it had never been heard of forcing this on Africans. But these bleaching products were the creations of the West. Because of this, the West faintly persuaded some naïve Africans to think and believe that white complexion was superior to black complexion. In this, the West has a problem.

Real superiority is in the nobility of the mind and action that add to the world development. That is the way of the world's great sages. You may wish to call this international patriotism. It is a streak available to all men across borders, and history abounds with many examples of this.

Nelson Mandela was a black man, with a noble character. His mind was bigger than those of his persecutors because theirs was prejudicial when his was unbiased and peaceful, taking the path of reconciliation in the midst of an enclave of racism. Was he not celebrated even by the whites for his good spirit which had elements of divinity? Therefore, Africans must love how God has formed them before they can be patriotic. It is then Africa will develop with its identity retained and maintained.

"Yes, it has become very necessary for me to do so," Matthew responded to his wife.

"You must have a reason for that, daddy," she said, squinting her eyes. Matthew tried blinking but a drop of tears splashed on his book. He looked tired for he barely slept for more than three hours every night.

"Oh, yes. I want to find out how these countries have progressed to where they are today."

"Tell me about your findings," she demanded, raising her head and looking silently into the space as if trying to find out reasons why such countries have developed.

"The common denominator of these countries is patriotism," Matthew responded, wishing that the minds of Africans will be transformed to have positive national and continental interests that will culminate into the general development of the continent.

"I think these countries have a mindset of commitment in all they do," Titi said.

"Mommy, one cannot be committed to the progress of one's country unless one is patriotic. That is why patriotism must be entrenched in Africa."

"Daddy, it is important that African patriotism be enshrined with love and respect for other continents," Titi said.

"Yes, our African founding fathers wanted Africa to live and walk in dignity with love and respect for other races of the world. They believed in the universal dignity of man."

"That is it! African patriotism must have a human face. The liberty and dignity of all races must not be tampered with in the pursuit for this."

"That is right," Matthew agreed.

"Daddy, it will be good if you go to visit your late friend's wife, Mercy. It's been a week since you were there."

"Yes, that is right. She still needs some encouragement even though she is strong."

"Daddy, public appearance is mostly different from the private. In private, she may be weeping even though it is now five months since Nelson is dead."

"You may be right. To lose a spouse is one of the most painful things that can ever happen to a person," Matthew agreed.

"Go, but don't stay long, please."

"Sure. I have been working on the address to be delivered at the forthcoming continental conference on patriotism," Matthew said.

***

Mercy was seated in the garden at the back of the house, her eyes fixed on an eagle gliding in the sky, calculating how to nose-dive successfully for her prey—a white chicken with few brown patches on its head that had been feeding around the garden. She was so lonely. The whole place was quiet. The birds were silent. They perched on the trees in the garden as if still mourning the death of Nelson. The day Nelson died was the last day they were heard twittering their melodies. It was as if they, too, were mourning along with the people. Nelson was, indeed, a great man to be mourned even by the birds.

***

"Peace unto this blessed home," Matthew pronounced as he entered Nelson's home.

"You are welcome, Matthew. Come to the garden," Mercy said, having recognized his voice. Suddenly, she heard a shriek from the chicken feeding nearby. The eagle, a giant bird able to carry a weight more than its own, had taken it away. Mercy saw it flying away with the chicken firmly grasped by its talons. A black hen came around cackling and fluttering its feathers in desperation to rescue the helpless chicken. Unfortunately, nature had not given her the ability to glide at high altitudes. The hen was obviously the chicken's mother. Mercy pitied the hen but there was nothing she could do to help. She thought of how the peace of the hen had been taken away by the eagle and likened this to how peace had been taken away from Africa by unpatriotic people. She believed that Africa's peace must be restored.

"Madam, how are you and the children doing?" Matthew interrupted her thought.

"We are doing well. Yes, we are," Mercy answered.

They sat silently for some time. It seemed the death of Nelson was coursing through their minds. The silence was broken by Mercy's voice.

"Matthew, Dr. Amodu Sekou, the Senegalese, visited us a week ago."

"Oh, that's nice to know. I learned he has the interest of Africa at heart."

"Yes, he has. He is selfless and agitates for national interests above personal. He is a patriot," Mercy confirmed.

"He is one of the silent preachers of patriotism. May God bless them abundantly," Matthew said and prayed. "I hope to get him work with me in preaching the gospel of patriotism."

"He told me that these days he has been told by his friends from five African countries that many bourgeois Africans are now thinking and speaking of patriotism more than ever before."

"That is very encouraging," Matthew said, becoming more attentive.

"Dr. Sekou said these progressive Africans are asking questions such as what was wrong with Africa even with all the abundant resources she has. You know they travel to many countries and see how developed they are."

"Yes, while waiting at terminals to board planes and while in the planes, that has always been one of the questions asked by Africans, madam."

"The language must now be action and no more questions. The starting point for this must be the renaissance of Africa," Mercy said, unhappy with Africa's underdevelopment.

"Something good will soon happen to Africa. We shall not continue like this."

"That is our hope," Mercy said.

"How is your husband's uncle?" Matthew asked and reminded Mercy of the cup the uncle broke the other time.

"He was here early in the morning to visit us. He is caring, especially since my husband died."

"That is lovely. That is patriotism. For one to love one's people is also patriotism to the country."

"Matthew, I hope you are planning very well for the continental conference. You know it will soon come." Matthew had told her about that during one of his visits to her.

"As a matter of fact, I want to leave now because of that."

"Go, please. Patriotism must be preached and entrenched effectively. That is the best tribute to be given to Nelson."

"Oh, yes. It is," Matthew said and he left.

Mercy watched him go, wishing she could see Nelson with him as she used to before he died. She sighed heavily, wondering about the essence of life. She thought of how man struggles beyond the necessities of life and strays into the region of primitive acquisition because of greed and lack of patriotism and then he dies, leaving the acquired material things, including the tent, his body, on the earth where they belong.

***

It was almost midnight on a Thursday; the village was gloomy and dark because it was a starless night as a result of clouds. Cold wind blew generously, unsettling trees and plants and the village smelled of wet earth as a result of showers in the afternoon. And now it wanted to rain again. Matthew was walking down the pond, hoping the rains would not start falling for him to visit the site where Nelson received the vision of the rising African patriots from. He made it a routine to visit the site weekly. This time around, the vision revealed to Matthew was that of the map of Africa, showing the rising African patriots in clusters of light shaped in human form all over Africa. They were many.

"Matthew, God is pleased with you because you are committed to the assignment given to you on patriotism for Africa," an angel of the LORD spoke to him.

"Thank you, the blessed one. God has enabled me to do this. He is the source of everything to me," he responded.

"Apart from the points of light, what do you see again on the map," the angel asked.

"Nothing, the blessed one," he responded.

"Yes, your eyes will be opened now. Can you tell me what you see now?"

"I can see skyscrapers all over Africa. I can also see people moving away from bodies of water. They are happy. Other people are also happy and are going round doing their work with passion, commitment and patriotism."

"Yes, that is right," the angel said.

"The blessed one, who are these people moving away from the bodies of water?"

"They are the people who have gathered to weep because of lack of patriotism in Africa. Nelson was given this vision when they were weeping."

"Oh, blessed one, this is sad."

"Now, they are moving away from these places with joy because they have seen glorious days coming to Africa."

"The blessed one, I can also see people from other continents standing by the edges of the African map, wanting to step in. What do they want?"

"They want to do business in Africa. They have seen the signs of a favorable economy in Africa. Africans in Diaspora, too, are among them."

"Will that actually come to reality, blessed one?"

"God will only tolerate this from you for now. If you allow your doubt on this to turn to faithlessness and unbelief, you will not experience this glorious epoch in the history of Africa," the angel warned.

"May the LORD be merciful on me and forgive me," Matthew cried.

"Why do you doubt? Have you not heard of Dubai?"

"I have, blessed one; it is in United Arab Emirate (UAE)."

"Was it not a desert now transformed into what it is today? This was achieved through passion, commitment and patriotism."

"I have heard about that, the blessed one."

"Any African country can do that. UAE made Dubai, even with her sub-tropical and arid climate, great in commerce and tourism."

"Yes, Lord."

"Dubai is now an attractive international economic hub for all people. Have you heard of Dubai Shopping Mall, of the Atlantis Hotel by the Arabian Gulf and of BurjKhalifa, the present tallest building in the world in downtown Dubai? Go and see the skyscrapers there. God help those who help themselves."

"Yes, the blessed one."

"Dubai is not shaken by the recent fall in oil prices. Proceeds from tourism are keeping that country financially buoyant."

The angel told Matthew that God allowed him to have that vision in a foggy weather to make him know that no matter the hindrance, patriotism had come to stay in Africa.

"Run to your home now. It is about to rain. Don't look back."

"Okay, the blessed one."

"When patriotism manifests in Africa, anyone that looks back desiring outdated ways will be found unfit to partake of its fruits. Do you get me?"

"Yes, sir; yes, the blessed one," Matthew responded, getting ready to run. He ran so fast like in a race. A wrap of money fell off his pocket but he still did not stop to pick it. Picking it would mean looking back and he will never go against the angel's instruction. What was a wrap of money compared to the fruits of patriotism that would soon adorn Africa?

Immediately Matthew stepped into his room, the rain fell generously. The rain had been restrained so that he could get home first.

***

"Matthew, God is pleased with you. You obeyed my instruction by not turning back to pick the wrap of money that fell off your pocket," the angel said to him in a dream that night.

He kept quiet and continued listening to the angel. "You know the money was secured in your pocket. I made it fall off your pocket to test your love for, and obedience to God. This was a trial and not temptation. You overcame it."

Matthew listened passionately. "Because of this, God will honour you beyond the shores of Africa. You are now a noble vessel in the hand of God for the good of Africa and the whole world."

***

In Durban, South Africa, the African conference on patriotism was held. South Africa was chosen as the venue so as to honour late Nelson Mandela, the patriotic icon. Speeches were delivered by many Africans with patriotism as their common pivot and theme. When it was time for Matthew to deliver his speech, the hall was quiet and still. Everyone was anxious to listen.

On the platform, he cleared his throat and began to deliver his paper with uncommon oratory.

MATTHEW (1967-)

"All protocols duly observed and respected. Today will ever be remembered with joy because we have gathered here as progressives to determine a glorious future for Africa through the instrument of patriotism. But what is patriotism? It is the love for one's country above personal interest even to the extent of paying the supreme price of giving up one's life for the survival of one's country. That is the way of the patriots of all great nations without racial segregation. Such patriots are the class of people that really understand these words on the marble by John F. Kennedy, *'Ask not what your country can do for you, but what you can do for your country.'*[1]Such noble people will never be satisfied until their countries are raised to majestic heights of patriotism that will culminate in their physical development with equity and justice reigning in them, letting the common good of mankind to be the umbrella for all, rich or poor, privileged or underprivileged, educated or uneducated, and leaders or followers. This kind of people also appreciate these words of John F. Kennedy; *'If a free society cannot help the many who are poor, it cannot save the few who are rich.'*[2]

The patriots are honourable people whose major fear is not the loss of their lives but their reputation. Honourable people will not eat until all are satisfied. The patriots are honourable people who will not sleep until others sleep. The patriots are noble people who will not rob their countries to enrich other countries. They are made in the mold of the first American President, George Washington who, in his inaugural addresses to the Congress on 30th April, 1789, said, "*.... By the article establishing the executive department, it is made the duty of the president to recommend to your consideration such measures as he shall judge necessary and expedient. The circumstances under which I now meet you will acquit me from entering in that subject further than to refer to the great constitutional charter under which you are assembled, and which, in defining your powers, designates the objects to which your attention is to be given. It will be more consistent with those circumstances and far more congenial with the feelings which actuate me, to substitute, in place of a recommendation of particular measures, the tribute that is due to the talents, the rectitude, and the patriotism which adorn the characters selected to devise and adopt them. In these honorable qualifications I behold the surest pledges that as on one side on local prejudices or attachments, no separate views nor party animosities, will misdirect the comprehensive and equal eye which ought to watch over this great assemblage of communities and interest, so, on another that the foundation of our national policy will be laid on the pure and immutable principles of private morality, and the preeminence of free government be exemplified by all the attributes which can win the affections of its citizens and command the respect of the world. I dwell on this prospect with every satisfaction which an ardent love for my country can inspire, since there is no truth more thoroughly established than that there exists in* *the economy and course of nature an indissoluble union between virtue and happiness; between duty and advantage; between the genuine maxims of an honest and magnanimous policy and the solid reward of public prosperity and felicity; since we ought to be less persuaded that the propitious smiles of Heaven can never be expected on a nation that disregards the eternal rules of order and right which Heaven itself has ordained; and since the preservation of the sacred fire of liberty and the destiny of the republican model of government are justly considered, perhaps, as deeply, as finally, staked of the experiment entrusted to the hands of the American people.*

"Besides the ordinary objects submitted to your care, it will remain with your judgment to decide how far an exercise of the occasional power delegated by the fifth article of the constitution is rendered expedient at the present juncture by the nature of objections which have been urged against the system, or by the degree of inquietude which has given birth to them. Instead of undertaking particular recommendations on this subject, in which I would be guided by no lights derived from official opportunities, I shall again give way to my entire confidence in your discernment and pursuit of the public good; for I assure myself that whilst you carefully avoid every alteration which might endanger the benefits of a united and effective government, or which ought to await the future lessons of experience, a reverence for the characteristic rights of freemen and regard for the public harmony will sufficiently influence your deliberations on the question how far the former can be impregnably fortified or the latter be safely and advantageously promoted.

"To the forgoing observations I have one to add, which will be most properly addressed to the House of Representatives. It concerns myself, and will therefore be as brief as possible. When I was first honoured with a call into the service of my country, then on the eve of an arduous struggle for its liberties, the light in which I contemplated my duty required that I should renounce every pecuniary compensation. From this resolution I have in no instance departed; and being still under the impressions which produced it, I must decline as inapplicable to myself any share in the personal emolument which may be indispensably included in a permanent provision for the executive department, and must accordingly pray that the pecuniary estimates for the station in which I am placed may during my continuance in it be limited to such actual expenditures as the public good may be thought to require..."[3]

The above speech is self-explanatory and very heart touching. It was from a heart that was lost completely in the knowledge of the supremacy of national interests above personal interests; a heart that knew real honour and dignity; a heart that was selfless and full of love for its country. It is our (the patriots') desire to see that African leaders and followers aspire for this noble character to make Africa great and we shall be there.

The other day, two weeks ago, I was in a secondary school to deliver a speech on patriotism. I did some historical analysis of the wonderful achievements of other countries that were at the same stage of development with some countries in Africa at independence. These countries are more developed than the African countries. As the students listened to the analysis, they wept. The assembly ground was thrown into confusion. When they finally gathered themselves, I told them that it is one thing to weep and it is another thing to act. I told them not to forget too easily after leaving the school, and that they must always remember it and take action to develop Africa. They chorused, *"we will not forget; we will not forget. Africa shall be great! Africa shall be great!"*

We that are gathered here today must put our words into action to set good examples for these children and the rest to emulate. We must stop all forms of selfish interests that hinder national or continental interests.

Finally, I am of the conviction that late George Washington's speech quoted above and these words; *"Ask not what your country can do for you, but what you can do for your country"* by late President John F. Kennedy have said it all as far as this issue of patriotism is concerned. Let us read and meditate on it and take action to entrench patriotism in Africa. With divine providence, we shall make Africa the darling of the world. Never will Africa be scorned anymore by any continent. We must work and work with commitment for this to be a reality.

Thank you so much for listening."

In attendance at the conference were participants from Britain; one of them was Mr. G. Clever, known all over the world as an activist who was against all forms of racial prejudice. He was even scorned at by some of his people for being anti-racist.

Mr. G. Clever was given an opportunity to deliver a goodwill message.

"All protocols are observed," began Mr. Clever.

"I am so glad for this opportunity to speak in this very crucial conference where worthy African sons are gathered for her progress. This is a commendable project and may God help us all.

We, the progressives in the West, are solidly behind you to ensure that patriotism is entrenched in Africa. We are not saying that in the West we do not have unpatriotic people; they are there but they have been overpowered by the patriots who are the majority. That is why we have developed our nations.

We, the progressives, are seriously fighting against all forms of racism. We must admit that we have many obstacles on our way in this noble fight but there is hope because, day by day, the concept of the universal dignity of man is progressively appreciated by more and more people in the West. This is because people are now thinking like the legendary French aviation pioneer author, Autoine de Saint-Exupery, who said *'I have no right to say or do anything that diminishes a man in his own eyes. What matters is not what I think of him, but what he thinks of himself. Hurting a man in his dignity is a crime.'*[4]

You are aware of how Africans are presently elected into parliaments in the West. This is as a result of this new and progressive thinking. We are all brothers and equal before God. I am not sermonizing, anyway.

However, I must advise you, Africans, to increase the capital of your patriotism. Africans should learn to resist any form of social, political or economic sabotage from either internal or external factors. I am from the West but I hate this sabotage. All of us, the progressives from the West, hate it. It is ugly, disgusting and humiliating. You must learn to love your continent for nobody, even I, will love your continent to the detriment of his own. For now, I wish you success in this noble aspiration. Thank you."

"This is a sincere goodwill message!" a man shouted from the crowd, applauding loudly.

There was loud ovation that left the people yearning for more messages like G. Clever's.

TWELVE

ᘓᘔ

Matthew gestured his desire to leave for school and his wife's face collapsed in anguish. She will miss him, she thought. She watched as he slowly put on his *made-in-Onitsha* pair of shoe. He had refused to wear anything foreign since he was commissioned to take over from Nelson Mamman. He had abandoned in a corner of his room two pairs of foreign made shoes— one Italian, the other made in China; half bag of rice imported from Thailand, cartons of match box made in India..., saying he would gradually do away with foreign things that can as well be produced in Africa. He would only buy foreign goods that were not and could not be produced in Africa. He said Africans must insist on fair world trade deals which would allow African products access to the global market without unnecessary barriers. He said that the World Bank, International Monetary Fund (IMF) and World Trade Organization (WTO) should work towards providing economic supports and grants to all economically weak nations without segregation based on political considerations.

"Daddy, your breakfast is ready," Titi said, placing the breakfast on the table. She knew it was patriotic doing things on time. She did her best to ensure her husband didn't go to work late, too.

Matthew mumbled a 'thank you' and walked smartly to the table.

"What do you intend to teach the class today?" Titi asked.

"History," he answered, though he planned to replace that with an issue on patriotism. Titi started to mop the floor of the living room adorned with made-in-Africa interiors. Matthew appreciated the unique African designs and decors, too.

***

"Class," Matthew began, "I am very excited to tell you this morning that the wind of patriotism is already blowing all over Africa," he said and looked through a window facing the western part of the classroom. He was gazing at the horizon to see the rising African patriots. They were already scattering all over Africa, manifesting their activities as ordained by God. He smiled and left the window, clapping his hands with joy to the amazement of the class. He was full of joy because of what he saw, the rising patriots.

"Sir, it seems you have a story on patriotism for us this morning," a student who had followed Nelson with keen interest and had himself been concerned about the economic stagnation of Africa, observed.

"I always have," he replied.

"Tell us, sir," the student said.

Matthew took a newspaper, rattle the phlegm in his throat and read out audibly to the class.

'*God has started blessing the efforts of the progressives in Africa who have been zealously preaching patriotism. We have learned that young workers in Uganda and Tanzania are imbibing the culture of going to the office in good time and are refusing to compromise public interest for personal interest.*'

"That is good news, sir," the student remarked.

"Yes, it is. Before I left my house this morning, I listened to the news on the radio," Matthew continued.

"What did you hear from it, sir?" Godiya, a dark and pretty girl asked.

"The reporter said that here in Nigeria, our country, there is an upsurge of patriotism in our young men."

"Tell us more, sir," Godiya said.

"Our young men are now going for noble values such as honesty, patriotism, hard work and time consciousness in all they do, as well as despising fraudulent activities."

"Sir, these could be the rising African patriots you told us about before," Godiya supposed, an aura of joy flooding her oval face.

"That is correct. They will be full of national pride. They will also give Africa face in international outlook. Yes, what do you want to ask?" Matthew asked, having noticed a student timidly raising his hand.

"It is not a question, sir," the student responded.

"What is it?"

"A friend of mine schooling in Ethiopia called two days ago to tell me that there is now an upsurge of patriotic activities in the country."

"Go on, I am listening," Matthew said, all eager to hear.

"The people are saying that Africans should be like the late Ethiopian Prime Minister, Meles Zenawi, who after a critical analysis refused economic policies wrongly prescribed for Ethiopia. Only the favourable ones should be accepted, taking into consideration the nature of the economic crisis and the conditions for the implementation of the prescribed policies."

"Yes, that is what we are saying. African leaders must be patriotic enough to resist prescription of wrong economic policies and neo-colonialism."

"Yes, that is how it should be, sir," the student agreed, looking satisfied.

"From Morocco, the country of late patriotic Ahmad Youssef, news is coming in that young engineers have formed an organization called Patriotic Engineers for Africa (PEA)," Matthew revealed.

"Sir, who will finance the various researches they will embark upon?" the student asked, saying a lot of money was needed for this.

"Before the government will get into it, the Engineers have agreed to make a lot of sacrifice for this. That is the way of the patriots. They always sacrifice for their countries' growth. They don't always leave everything for the government to do." He told them those words of John F. Kennedy, *'Ask not what your country can do for you, but what you can do for your country.'"*

Catherine Samson, the girl sitting close to the window that Matthew had been staring through raised her hand up, wanting to speak. She was allowed.

"Sir," she began, "It seems many positive things have started happening in Africa."

"Yes, Catherine, a new dawn is manifesting in Africa. We will be there very soon."

"Where, sir?" Catherine asked.

"The level other continents have reached in patriotism, engineering, technology and economic progress," Matthew explained with joy.

"Sir," Catherine continued, "my father told my mom yesterday that many Africans are withdrawing their money from foreign banks back to their countries."

"Yes, I know about that. A friend of mine called in from Kenya last week to inform me that many rich Kenyans are withdrawing their money from commercial banks in the West. They are bringing them back home to help in developing their country. This is what is happening all over the continent.

"Catherine, you seem to be struggling to raise your hand. Do you have something again to say?" Matthew asked, turning swiftly to write these words on the black board; EVEN THE RACISTS' MISGUIDED SENSE OF SUPERIORITY WILL COME BACK HOME.

"Yes, sir. My father also told my mom that in South Africa, in Botswana and in the Democratic Republic of Congo, the middle class is becoming more patriotic by thinking more of national interests above ethnic interests. He said there are manifesting signs of progress in those countries," Catherine added.

Matthew raised his head, closed his eyes and held his hands folded at his back, moving his nose as if he was sniffing the fragrance of something. He later told the class that it was the fragrance of patriotism blowing all over Africa that he was sniffing. He told the class that all that they were listening to that morning was the manifest presence of the rising African patriots that was gradually taking over the affairs of Africa.

"Sir, who are the racists that will come back home?"Stephen James, a student, asked.

"The racists are people who treat other races as inferior humans even though no race is superior to others."

"Are they coming back home to Africa?" Stephen James asked, finding it hard to understand what Matthew meant.

"No, Stephen; you have gotten it wrong!"

"Kindly explain, sir," Stephen James pleaded.

"Once again, the racists are the people that treat other races as if they are inferior; that is racial prejudice. Some people in the West treat Africans that way. Even some Africans have racist inclinations. Their misguided sense of superiority will come back home one day and the true brotherhood of all mankind will ensue. I must say, as I have said before, that there are progressive whites who believe in the equal worth of all men. They are the friends of Africa."

"I can understand, sir," Stephen James said, looking demoralized and thinking of how racism was a global disgrace to mankind and how bad it must be in the eyes of God.

"Let me tell you a story, class. There was an African-American called Martin Luther king, Jr. He was a civil right activist in America where Africans were heavily subjected to the evil of racism. He made a vow one day to his mother when he was young.

'...when I get to be a man, I'm gonna hit this thing and I'm gonna hit it hard.... Mother, there is no such thing as one people being better than another. The Lord made all of us equal, and I'm gonna see to that.'[1] He was an African-American patriot in Diaspora. He fulfilled the vow he made to his mother by fighting for the civil rights of African-Americans.

"Sir, he was a great man that we young men should emulate."

"Yes, Stephen, especially emulating the doctrine of nonviolent confrontations which he took after from M. K. Gandhi. He won the Nobel Peace Prize in 1964. In the struggle for the freedom of the African-Americans he once said to the people, *'I want you to go home and put down your weapons. We cannot solve this problem through retaliatory violence. We must love our white brothers, no matter what they do to us. We must make them know we love them.... We must meet hate with love.'*[2]

That is also the stance of our late great patriot, Nelson Mamman. I am also of that school of thought."

"But, sir, it is not all the whites that practice racial prejudice," Stephen James observed.

"Oh yes! I said that earlier. We have many progressives in the West. For example, Glen Smiley supported the Montgomery bus boycott occasioned by the racial maltreatment of Mrs. Rosa Parks by a bus driver. Many whites with a conscience joined the blacks for the civil rights match in Washington, D.C," Matthew sighed deeply and ended discussions on the topic.

A green fly flew into the class and perched on Matthew's forehead. It must have come from the cows grazing at the school boundary. The wind was blowing dry dust outside the classroom as it hummed over the classrooms and through the school compound. Matthew felt the breeze in the class and the fly on his forehead but did nothing about it. He was engrossed thinking of how the Nigerian flag at the entrance of the house of late Nelson was torn and the pole bent because it wasn't lowered to mourn the death of Ahmed Youssef, the Moroccan. He thought of Nelson and his zeal to see patriotism reign over Africa. He remembered how Nelson prevented him from throwing a stone at a dove that perched on the tree whose shade, he, Nelson and Kweku were standing under. He remembered how he carelessly dropped the stone on Kweku's foot and how Kweku screamed and writhed in pains; how the dove flew over the river and perched on a dry tree. He recalled the vision he had of Nelson's death and how he felt.

By the time he turned to face the class again, his face was emotional and the students knew it.

"Stephen, what is it again?" Stephen still wanted to know more about the racists coming back home.

Matthew laughed weakly and said, "I mean the white people, great in number, are beginning to understand the evil of racial discrimination and are now appreciating the equality and dignity of all races. The progressive whites are preaching this now more than in any other time in history. But…,"

"But what, sir?" Stephen James asked.

"Africans must move ahead to imbibe the culture of patriotism that will develop Africa. It is because we have refused to make progress in many aspects that this racial prejudice is still used to hold us down. Thank God for the patriotic stories we are now hearing from all over Africa."

"Sir," a boy called Cletus said. "I had a dream last night in which I saw white birds from the West and the East flying into Africa. In the dream, I saw bright points of light all over Africa. Africa was serene and graceful. A man in white clothes with eyes burning like wild fire told me that the white birds flying into Africa from the West and the East are the whites who have noticed the potential glory in Africa and are coming to partake in it. The man told me that patriotism will reign over Africa enshrouding it like a garment."

"And what again?"

"The man just disappeared into the air."

Matthew laughed hysterically. He kept quiet and laughed again. The class was surprised and at the same time confused about his laughter. When he stopped laughing he asked the class, "Who do you think was the man Cletus saw in the dream."

Some said it was Ahmad Youssef. Some said it was Nelson Mamman. Some said it was Nelson Mandela. Some said it was Martin Luther King Jr. Some said it was W.E.B. Du Bios and some said it was Booker T. Washington, a former Virginian slave who encouraged African-Americans to pursue educational and economic progress by *'lifting others up as we climb."*

The students had been taught about all these patriots.

As Matthew mumbled some indistinct words, he droops his head, fixing it on the earth and then nodded gradually. His face suddenly turned gloomy with rippling sadness all over his countenance. He had been having emotional instability lately, especially when he thought of his late friend and mentor Nelson

Mamman. But for Nelson's heroic feats, he was consoled greatly.

"What is the matter with you, sir?" Cletus asked.

"These were great patriots who loved a good name over materialism. They were men refined for heavenly things. They loved Africa and Africans more than their lives, "Matthew replied, shaking his head as he remembered the words of Du Bois concerning the founding, in May 1910, of the National Association for the Advancement of Colored People (NAACP) which says; *'to promote equality of rights and eradicate caste or race prejudice among the citizens of the United States'* and *'the interest of colored Americans.'*[3]

He was also hurt as he remembered the separate but equal South and the ghetto north where, in both places the African-Americans were racially discriminated for being blacks and relegated to the status of second-class citizens. But when he remembered the admonition of Martin Luther King, Jr. that the African-Americans should meet the forces of hate with the power of love and that they must learn to love the white man, he became hopeful.

He told the class that none of their answers was correct. He told them that the man Cletus saw in the dream was an angel of the LORD who had given them (Ahmad Youssef, Nelson Mamman and himself) the vision of the rising African patriots that were now manifesting with patriotism all over Africa and would soon be all over the world to knit the hearts of all mankind together regardless of race in unity.

From South Sudan, Matthew received a call from Frances Kish, a tall and dark complexioned man who was one of the people in the South Sudanese team that attended the burial of Nelson Mamman. He was from the financial community but he had been very patriotic in opposing financial policies that were imposed on African countries to exploit them. He had been advocating for the integration of Africans into the mainstream of technical skills by the western countries that operate in Africa rather than being continuously left wanting in technological advancement. He wept over how some Africans were still helping people from other countries to ravage Africa economically and to determine the political destiny of Africa. He had, on many occasions, expressed his feelings on how capitalism— though it causes hard work and innovations, destabilized communal labour in Africa, replacing it with selfish tendencies. However, he frowned at the deception of the communists and called on Africans to be patriotic enough to return to the great days of communalism. The call he made to Matthew was to tell him of how his wish was gradually being achieved all over Africa; news of patriotic acts are pouring in from all over Africa.

That morning, Matthew answered Mr. Frances Kish's call with an indescribable joy in his heart. The call reminded him of the rising African patriots and how their coming would shut out ethnic and regional differences. He smiled for the thought of it was comforting enough.

"Good day, Mr. Matthew," Frances Kish responded after Matthew greeted him, his voice brimming with excitement.

"How is South Sudan?"

"Fine, very fine; a new dawn of patriotism is rippling all over my country, South Sudan. Regional and ethnic loyalties are crumbling before the indomitable force of national patriotism."

"What is it that is actually happening, my good friend?" Matthew asked, praising God in his mind for the New World Order that is gradually being entrenched in Africa.

"The different groups fighting in our country are now becoming patriots."

"Yes, I am listening."

"That is right! Right now, they are laying down their arms for patriotic resolution of conflict. In Mali and other seething African countries, it is the same story," Mr. Kish narrated, wishing that Africa would reach a stage whereby her export dominates her imports to enable economic advancement.

"Is there any other thing again, Mr. Kish?"

"Yes, young people are now asking questions on why Africa is lagging behind in development. They seem to have a new value system— a positive one— different from the conservative and crude one."

"They are the manifesting African patriots. They will restore the dignity of Africa everywhere upon the face of the earth."

"Yes, Matthew, they will not rest until they take Africa to great heights. They are passionately determined and divinely motivated."

"They will not sleep as many of us have been sleeping. They know, as James Allen says, *'The heights by great men reached and kept were not attained by sudden flight; but they, while their companions slept, were toiling upward in the night'*" Matthew agreed and quoted, unable to remember the source. He was not comfortable with this.

"They will resist unnecessary and restrictive economic policies that will arrest the development of

Africa. Pollsters have glaringly shown this tendency. This wind of patriotism is swiftly blowing all over Africa."

"Yes, Mr. Kish, it is. Even pregnant women are telling exciting stories of how babies in their wombs leap with joy whenever the word patriotism is mentioned. That is the language they will understand and like to hear when they are born. They, too, are among the rising African patriots that will continue to manifest until Africa is full of them."

"Wait, Matthew, let me answer a call from Rwanda. Just hold on, please," Mr.Kish pleaded.

***

"Yes, M.K, how are you and Rwanda?"

"I am fine, and you? Rwanda is becoming good, Mr. Kish.

"I am doing well!"

"I just want to tell you that the new leaders of our country are doing a lot of wonderful work here. All their actions are for the public good. They are wonderful."

"That is the story around Africa now. The following people, Ahmad Youssef of Morocco, Nelson Mamman of Nigeria (both of blessed memory) and one Matthew, also of Nigeria, saw this coming in a vision. We thank God that we are partakers of this."

"Oh, yes; oh yes; glory be to God," M.K. said

"M.K, I will call you later. I have kept somebody on hold all this while."

***

"Matthew," Mr. Kish called, "nobody should doubt that a new era is dawning on Africa."

"What is it?"

"One of the crusaders for patriotism in Rwanda named M. K told me that the young leaders in Rwanda are patriotically doing a lot of wonderful work for the country."

"We are grateful to God. He speaks and fulfils," Matthew said, still remembering the vision of the rising patriots.

"What is happening in Nigeria now, Matthew?"

"Both Christians and Muslims are now realizing the foolishness in killing one another due to political brainwashing. They now have a new patriotic mentality. Youths from the south and from the north are teaming up to patriotically take up political and social responsibilities from political dinosaurs. Things are changing for good."

"The bones of our founding fathers, the bones of 'Ahmad Youssef', the bones of Nelson Mandela, the bones of 'Nelson Mamman' and the bones of all dead African patriots will now lie in their graves peacefully. Their vision for Africa is becoming a reality," Mr. Kish said.

"Yes, they will smile because the time has come when Africans will walk everywhere upon the face of the earth with dignity," Matthew said, shedding tears of joy, and saying good bye to Mr. Kish.

"I will hear from you soon, Matthew," Mr. Kish responded.

***

Matthew's chair dangled as he sank into it. The class was silent. They had heard the discussion

Matthew had with Mr. Frances Kish. They were happy for Africa, too.

Matthew pulled out from his folder an old and crumpled document given to him some years back by the late Nelson Mamman, who himself had gotten it from a silent and unknown patriot. On the paper it was written:

> *"By the rivers of Africa and on her mountaintop, we sat and wept when we remembered the arrested development of Africa by the forces of slavery and colonialism aided by some unpatriotic Africans. We wept the more when we realized how the patriotic dream of our founding fathers have been destroyed by neo-colonialism and aided, in some cases, by unprogressive Africans for selfish reasons against the society. As we wept, we asked of who could restore the dignity of Africa. God gave us a vision without explanation. We saw in the horizon a sparkling 'cloud' rising to spread all over Africa. We desired the meaning of this vision like a baby craves for milk, but the Mighty One told us that the meaning will not be given to us but to another generation. We pressed no more but we were comforted by this vision. Africa will rise again."*

Matthew read the paper and remembered it was to Ahmed Youssef and Nelson Mamman the meaning of that vision was given, but they were denied witnessing its manifestation. He thanked God for letting him see the vision and its early manifestation. He thanked God for His faithfulness and screamed in praise while the class looked on with amazement at this strange behavior.

"Africa, take your rightful place among other continents of the world," and he uttered the timeless words of one of the great patriots of Africa in Diaspora, Martin Luther King Jr. The class was so quiet and attentive; you could hear nothing but his authoritative voice.

"Nothing could be more tragic than for men to live in these revolutionary times and fail to achieve the new attitudes and the new mental outlooks that the new situation demands."[4]

With these insightful words, he urged the class and all progressive Africans to flow with the new revolutionary tide of patriotism so as to bring glory to Africa.

REFERENCES

Chapter One

1. M. K. Gandhi; *The Story of my Experiment with Truth*, p. 163

Chapter Two

1. *Benajmin Disrael: Inspire The Giant Within* by Andras Lara, p. 58.
2. John C. Maxwell: *The Winning Attitude, Your Pathway to Success*, pp. 152 – 152.
3. James Allen: *As A Man Thinketh*, p. 200.

Chapter Five

1. Nelson Mandela: The News, Vol. 41, No. 23, 16 December, 2013, p. 28.

Chapter Six

1. Ngugi waThiong'o. New African, 47th Year, December 2013, No. 534, p. 94.
2. Lord Mansfield: Historical Flashback, Vol. 3, No. 2, Jan. 15 – Feb. 11, 2014, p. 3.
3. Donald T. Phillips: Martin Luther King, Jr. On Leadership, pp. 172 – 173.
4. Donald T. Phillips: Martin Luther King, JrOn Leadership, pp. 211 – 214.
5. Nelson Mandela: The News, Vol. 41, No. 23, 16 December, 2013, p. 28.
6. Nelson Mandela: The News, Vol. 41, No. 23, 16 December, 2013, p. 28.
7. Dr. Williams Edward Burgherdt, New African No. 534, December, 2013, p. 85.

Chapter Seven

1. Tito Alai: New African, 48th Year, April 2014, No. 538, p. 57.

Chapter Eight

1. James Allen: *As a Man Thinketh*, pp. 79 – 80.
2. James Allen: *As A Man Thinketh*, p. 83.

Chapter Ten

1. Apostle Paul: 1 Corinthians 4 : 6 - 7

Chapter Eleven

1. *John F. Kennedy: The World's Greatest Speeches* Compiled by Vijaya Kumar, p. 100.
2. John F. Kennedy: Same source as 1 above, p. 98.
3. George Washington: Same source as 1 and 2 above, pp. 193 – 195.
4. Antoine de Saint-Exupery: *How to Win Friends and Influence People by Dale* Carnegie, p. 226.

Chapter Twelve

1. Martin Luther King, Jr. On Leadership by Donald T. Phillips, p. 29.
2. Martin Luther King, Jr. On Leadership by Donald T. Phillips, pp. 49 – 50.
3. Du Bois: The same source as 1 and 2 above, p. 18.
4. Martin Luther King, Jr. On Leadership by Donald T. Phillips, P. 134.s

www.ingramcontent.com/pod-product-compliance
Lightning Source LLC
Chambersburg PA
CBHW061230170626
46809CB00007B/2597

* 9 7 8 9 7 8 5 5 6 1 3 3 3 *